ALL ABOUT FOREVER

ALL OR NOTHING SERIES
BOOK THREE

ASHLEY ERIN

All About Forever

Copyright © 2019 by Ashley Erin

Cover Design by Vanilla Lily Designs

Editing by Missy Borucki

Proofreading by Virginia Tesi Carey

Interior Design: Heritage Creek Formatting

CHAPTER ONE

Ryan

"You're kidding, right?" I stare at Dane, frustration building as he gives me his "are you an idiot?" look, as though the bomb he's just dropped on me is an every day occurrence.

"You knew this was coming!" His tone is calm, despite the frustrated look on his face.

"How could you do that without consulting me first? We weren't through discussing the job description and necessary credentials for the position. I can't believe you went ahead and made this decision without me." I glare at my little brother. Completely unfazed by my outburst, he tilts back in my chair, his eyes tracking me as I pace in front of my desk, irritation making my feet move.

It was such a pleasant morning too, until he came sauntering in with his "good news." Things at the house have been picking up speed again and I woke up to a morning blow job that made letting the chick from last night stay over worthwhile. Dane's sigh of utter exasperation interrupts the memory, drawing my attention back to the conversation I just want to end.

"Ryan, I tried. You're the one who chose not to be a part of the hiring process, to drag out or cancel meetings we'd planned to discuss hiring someone. We sat down as a family and discussed this, agreed it was the best decision for the business. You were taking too long to come up with your 'criteria,' so I went ahead because I know you well enough to know the qualifications you want in a partner. You're out of commission for ten weeks, and that's only if you do as you're told. Ten weeks is too long for your clients to wait for their horses' hooves to be trimmed." Dane's lips pull back into a firm line as he straightens, his posture brokering no room for argument. "You bring in thirty-five percent of this ranch's income. We can't afford to lose that, especially in this economy."

"My clients. Not yours. Mine. You shouldn't have made this decision behind my back," I holler, slamming my left hand onto the counter, ignoring his very valid point.

I had assumed, wrongly apparently, that if I put it off they would drop the subject and let me deal with my time off the way I wanted—to have a few of my farrier contacts take on my clients while I'm out of commission. It never crossed my mind that Dane would go ahead and hire someone without my input.

"Behind your back? You can't be serious! I've been waiting for you to come around, this wasn't some random thought, this is a serious decision that needed to be dealt with immediately. You refused to, so as the family appointed operations manager of the ranch, I took it upon myself. I invited you to all the interviews. You made the choice not to be involved, no one else. This is on you. Reese has ten years of experience as a farrier. We didn't hire someone who is fresh out of shoeing school. Ten years. That's two years longer than you." Dane's voice is exasperated, his brow creasing as he gestures wildly at me. "We can't risk losing clients, and we definitely can't sacrifice the money that continuing to serve those clients will bring in."

I know what he's saying makes sense, but I built my business from scratch, my reputation in this community is the result of painstaking work, long hours, and a dedication to improving my craft, including staying on top of new research that comes out and exploring whether it's something I want to incorporate into my practice. The idea of anyone else coming in with their own ideas and trying to take advantage of the fact I'm out of commission, it's too much for me to handle.

"Just remember, I'm still the boss. This guy needs to do things my way. I also reserve the right to fire him should he not work out." I'm firm on this point, the rational part of my brain knows Dane would never hire anyone he thought would compromise our name and business, but that part of me isn't louder than the side that hates the idea of sharing my space and my clients.

He coughs, and if I didn't know better I would think he's coughing to cover a laugh, odd considering he's about ready to rip my head off.

"Reese is under contract for three months, in that time I expect you to be fair and reasonable. Give this a chance, Ryan." He gives me a pointed look.

Rolling my eyes, I move to cross my arms, muttering a curse when my bulky cast gets in the way. "He has the job, that's his chance. He needs to earn my respect as well as my clients."

"You're going to give this a chance. I'm serious. Don't make me bring Mom and Dad into this. Reese is coming Sunday afternoon to tour the shop to prepare for Monday." He continues to speak, but I'm not even listening. I have a few days to adjust to the idea that someone is coming in and becoming the face of my business.

It's been on the table for a while to hire an associate farrier, but my siblings have allowed me to delay, saying we didn't need to add anything to our plate. Especially since Dane and Emma are planning a wedding and Lia's going to be off soon to rest during the remainder of her pregnancy and for three months afterward.

Now this damn arm has brought on the inevitable and I can't even do it my way.

Dane shouting my name draws my attention back to him. "Do I need to be there to make sure you behave?" His damn smirk is back, causing my face to fall into a glower.

Glaring at him, I don't bother to give him a response and just point at my door. He shoves up from my desk and leaves, his laughter taunting me. "This is going to be good for all of us, you may as well get over your tantrum now, it will make life easier." His taunt trails off as the door closes with a bang. Narrowing my eyes, I glare at the space he just left behind. Why do I get the feeling he's keeping something from me?

Sunday morning is spent cleaning my already spotless shop. It's never been this clean or as organized. Well, maybe it was when I first set it up, but I'm sure that lasted only a day or two. The rectangular room usually has at least a little dirt on the ground from my boots, or some tools scattered throughout. Maybe a new box of horseshoes.

My desk is never tidy, there's always something covering it, even if it's the week's invoices and accounting sheet filled out and ready for Dane. Since I couldn't do anything else, I finally incorporated a filing system, something I'd been avoiding but no longer had any reason to ignore. I also transitioned my billing to strictly electronic versus paper. All this time spent in the office and not out with my horses has made me a crabby bastard.

Ever since the doctor told me I couldn't work for at least two months, I've felt trapped and the only thing I could do to cope was clean. Now, it's too spotless. I like a tidy workspace, but this is a little overdone. It's a constant reminder that I'm not working, a reminder that I'm essentially useless to my family business. Kicking my desk, I curse.

People need to learn to communicate. That damn horse knew exactly what he was doing when he kicked me, and they knew he would do it, the lack of surprise on their faces when it happened was all the evidence I needed. A few words of warning would've been enough to prevent this broken arm. I'm more than willing to work with a tough horse—holding their hoof in a different way or working through their anxiety —but the owners didn't want to pay me my hazard fee. That level of disregard for my safety is now costing my family significantly more than the hundred-dollar charge for working with potentially dangerous horses.

I circle the room for the tenth time as I wait until this Reese dude my brother hired shows up, and all it's doing is putting me in a foul mood. Which doesn't bode well for my professionalism. We're a good-natured family, typically, but I can't seem to shake this cloud hanging over me. My work is my life and being unable to contribute is wrecking me. My siblings have been avoiding me, aside from the mandatory breakfast Lia has imposed, and I can't say I blame them. I'm a miserable ass right now. I don't even like being in my own company.

Sunlight streams in when the door opens, the silhouette of a woman fills the frame. The light shining in from behind her highlights her curves and creates almost a halo around the top of her head. Turning, I watch with interest as she pauses, clearly taking stock of the space I'm so proud of.

"I'm sorry, we're closed today, but I could schedule you in. We're not booking for a couple weeks though." My voice is friendly as my lips curl into a grin. Tucking my good hand in my pocket, I plant myself on the edge of my desk. It's not often I have a walk-in client, especially on a Sunday.

She shuts the door, so I can finally view her clearly, her expression is friendly as she strides toward me with her hand out. She's cute, with wavy auburn hair and beautiful hazel eyes. My grin turns into a smirk as I check her out. The form-fitting jeans she's wearing accentuate mouth-watering curves, a plaid button up is tied at her waist and as she walks, I catch glimpses of a smooth stomach and perfect belly button. My lips quirk even more after my quick assessment, maybe she can brighten my mood. Her eyes scan me with the familiar hint of feminine interest, her cheeks flushing a little when my smirk becomes a full-on grin. I know the look in her eyes, I see it regularly before I bring a woman home. I wonder if we'd have enough time for a quick tryst before Reese shows up. My office has a decent amount of surface area we could—

"Hi, I'm Reese. I'm your new associate farrier." She gives me a friendly smile, the heated interest gone so fast I wonder if I imagined it. My grin falls as I stare at her before glancing down to her extended hand. I can feel my forehead crease and I'm positive I look completely bewildered.

"You're Reese?" My voice is incredulous, and I still haven't taken her hand. Locking eyes with her, I frown in denial. "That's impossible."

Her hand remains steady, the friendly smile holding firm. She's not wavering under my scowl. "I assure you, it's not impossible. I didn't bring my birth certificate, but I can show you my driver's license if you need confirmation. Dane let me know you were unavailable for my interview, but when I was hired, he said he'd let you know I was coming today and that he would apprise you to my qualifications. I have ten years of experience as a farrier, two of which were spent apprenticing with Roy Gardner, and the last eight on my own. Dane has my resume, but I have another copy in my truck if you need it."

Her hand stays put the entire time she talks, her voice steady and confident as she waits for me to accept her gesture, but my mind is spinning out of control. Why didn't Dane tell me Reese is a woman? I called her a guy several times, giving him plenty of time to correct me. Pursing my lips, it dawns on me that he omitted that piece of information on purpose, his smirk finally makes sense. He's going to pay for this.

I don't doubt she's skilled, but I try to limit my time spent with members of the opposite sex to my family members, clients, and the occasional one-night stand. It's not that I'm incapable of being around women, I'm not a jackass—most of the time—it's that I prefer to choose when and where I incorporate people into my life, and work is not that place.

I've always loved how solitary my job is, the quiet of my workshop, and now I'm obligated to share it with someone. I don't want to be stereotypical, but I find women tend to want to talk more, fill the silence which means letting them into your circle. That scares me, the last time I let a woman get close to me, she broke my heart.

Slowly, I reach my hand out and grasp hers, scowling even harder when my body reacts with eagerness to her touch. Her skin is smooth and silky soft, missing the scrapes and cuts that cover my skin, telling me it's been a while since she's worked. Her handshake is firm, strong, which at least fills me with hope that she has the strength for this job.

"Roy, huh?" I have a lot of respect for Roy, so I make a

mental note to call him after this joke of a tour is over. Her hand is small, mine envelops it, and as she draws it away, I feel the need to flex out my fingers, the smooth texture of her skin imprinting on mine. When was the last time I held a woman's hand in mine? I can't even remember, it's been so long.

"Yes, two years. He typically only keeps students on for one year, but he hired me as an assistant for the second." Her voice is full of pride, and when she smiles it's full of affection for the old man. He's not really that old, I just like to tease him, but he is one of the top farriers in North America. He tours around to different training programs and offers prestigious apprenticing opportunities, taking no more than three apprentices a year.

"I see. Well, since Dane went out of his way to hire you and plan this tour, let's get started." She doesn't react to my less than thrilled tone, which irks me. I want her to quit, back away and exit my shop. I was already against this idea to start with, but there is something about her that makes me even more resistant. Something in her smile and a twinge in my stomach when those hazel eyes meet my gaze. When she looks at me, her expression shifts to one I can only describe as analytical, there's something in the depth of her gaze that makes me feel exposed.

"This is my shop, I don't tend to stray from here often. Everything is organized *exactly* as I want it. I'm strict about putting tools and supplies back precisely where they were found as I've spent years trying to arrange everything in the most convenient and useful way possible. I'm assuming you have your own tools." I grunt in response to her nod. "Dane requested I clear a spot for you, so it's over there." Gesturing to a small cabinet in the back corner, I wait on an impatient sigh when she goes to check it out, once again without responding to my rudeness. It doesn't take her long before she's turning back toward me, her expression carefully neutral.

"Let's get on with it then." I don't ask if it's sufficient, I know she can make it work. Leading her outside, I point to Lia's clinic. "My sister, Lia, runs Hyatt Equine Therapy out of there. She does massage, chiropractic, and rehabilitation."

Reese walks beside me, taking in everything without a word. Glancing at her from the corner of my eye, I can't help but take in more of her features. I was wrong when I first saw her; she's not cute, she's stunning.

This is going to suck ass. I don't work well with anyone but my family, hence starting my business as a farrier. I'm my own boss and the only people I deal with are my clients. It's easy to put on a smile for them, but I hate fakeness and refuse to put on a charade for anyone else. Hopefully she has tough skin because I don't sugarcoat anything.

Leading her through the barn which houses six stalls, a tie stall, a tack room, a wash stall, a small arena, and a pool, we exit the facility to the back where the pens are. Lia currently has six horses staying for rehabilitation, they're all in their own corrals that are set to their individual needs.

One of the horses pops his head over the fence as we pass, blowing out a happy sigh when I scratch his neck.

"Most of this space is part of Lia's program. On occasion we work together rehabilitating a horse with laminitis or other issues that I can help with, but typically I stay out of her way. She has a student coming to learn, Nella. Lia has offered her a full-time position which will begin in August, so she doesn't need me much anymore. Nella, her daughter, and her sister are moving into the house down the road there."

We head back inside, Reese standing as I sit in my chair and lean back, eyeing her warily. I guess I should have brought one in here for her, but I didn't think of it. I add that to my list of things to do once she leaves.

She still hasn't said much except the odd soft hum as she

takes in our facility. It's state of the art and I can tell she wishes I would have let her check things out more closely. It's too bad for her that she's caught in the crosshairs of a family disagreement. They don't happen often, but then again, Dane doesn't often try to impose his "business sense" on my side of the family business.

"I need you to fill out some forms, including some amendments to the initial contract you signed with Dane. I believe you've discussed the changes with him, but we can go over them again if you like. Once the rest of the paperwork is filled out we'll go over our schedule for the week. I'm going to be blunt because honesty is the best policy, you were hired against my will. My clients expect a specific level of work, and my business is tied to my family business and the Hyatt name. I will not tolerate inadequate workmanship."

Tilting back in my chair, I watch as she narrows her eyes slightly, her nostrils flaring. This is the first time I've seen a physical reaction to my unpleasant attitude. She pulls her shoulders back and fixes me with a serious look, her eyes blazing. I'd be lying if I said my cock didn't harden at the sight, the slight flush on her cheeks similar to the flush I imagine she'd get if she were one of my hookups.

"Mister Hyatt, I've been in this business since I was twenty-four years old. I'm used to the attitude that because I'm a woman I can't do this job as well as my male colleagues, but I assure you that I work hard and provide a quality service. I have no doubt that I will be a positive representative for you and your family." Her tone is firm, but polite as she puts me in my place. Her manner professional and completely understandable given my attitude. Sadly, she seems to have thick skin when it comes to dealing with assholes, because that's what I'm being, and her response wouldn't warrant me firing her. I was hoping with that red hair of hers maybe she would have the temper to match.

Her words rankle me though, I don't give a flying rat's ass that she's a woman. I would be treating a man that walked in here the same way. Granted, the fact that she's a woman is inconvenient, but only because my cock has been semi-erect since I first saw her, a troublesome side effect to the fact that my body finds her incredibly attractive. Combining that with the fact that she seems to have a take-no-shit attitude, and I can tell if I let myself I would probably like her.

"You think I'm angry that Dane hired a woman?" Laughing harshly, I shove my chair back as I stand, ignoring it when it tips over. Pressing the palm of my good arm onto the surface of my desk, I lean forward and hold her gaze. "I couldn't care less if you're a man, woman, or purple alien. What I care about is having to surrender MY clients and MY business over to someone while I deal with this." I lift my broken arm.

Her eyes drop to the white cast covered in doodles that Lia's assistant's daughter drew all over it, her lips twitching as she fights a smirk.

"I like to work alone, if I didn't I would've hired someone two years ago, the moment I had to turn away my first client. I don't like to relinquish control and the idea of handing you my entire client roster is something I can't even think about right now. So, fill out the paperwork and don't categorize me with sexist assholes who feel threatened by a beautiful woman."

Sliding the folder across the table, I slam a pen down on top of it, bend to right the chair and walk away so she can sit down at my desk if she wants.

My phone is in my hand before she takes a seat.

Me: Why didn't you tell me Reese is a woman?

Dane: Does it matter?

Me: Not in the I care either way sense, but a little forewarning would've been nice. I'm still against this idea. I think I can still work, I just have to be careful.

Dane: You're kidding, right?

Me: No… But I suppose I can deal until my arm is healed.

Dane: Dude, we've hired her permanently, I told you that. Her three-month contract has a permanency clause. If she gets through probation, she's here for good. You're turning clients away, this way we don't have to… didn't you listen to a word I said when we discussed this? Or, you know, read the contract I forwarded to you?

Staring at his text, I glance over at Reese who's bent over the paperwork, her lips moving slightly as she reads. Her dark auburn hair falls over one of her shoulders, the soft waves a little unruly, like she was running her hands through them. Her hair shines in the muted light; the silky looking strands would look beautiful wrapped around my fist. Shutting down the fantasy, I widen my stance and focus back on my phone, dialling Dane.

"Ryan." His voice is resigned.

"I thought you were going to hire someone on a contract basis, and then decide to offer a permanent position if the person worked out. I may not be completely on board with this, but I do remember that." I fight to keep my voice low, glancing over to where she's still reading. I'm impressed she's taking the time, so many people sign things without understanding what exactly they're agreeing to.

He sighs and I can picture him scrubbing his hand over his

face, those creases in his forehead becoming more pronounced the more annoyed he gets with me. "Reese *is* contracted for the three months, but we made sure she knew that the opportunity is there for something permanent. That's the only way we could get her. That and offer her Lia's apartment in the clinic."

Hanging up on my brother, I squeeze the phone until my knuckles turn white.

How did I forget that part? The ruckus over the past week as they added an exterior door to the apartment has been infuriating. A constant reminder that I had someone not only invading my business, but my home as well.

And, now that I think of it, why would someone with ten years of experience want to work under someone else rather than maintaining their own business? Especially when I do have two years less experience than she does.

I hear her clear her throat, so I return to my desk and glance over her paperwork.

Just as she took the time to read her contract, I take the time to read her answers, taking the opportunity to learn a little more about her. She's thirty-four, five years older than me. Her previous employment was her own business. And she didn't list an emergency contact.

So many questions arise from just her employee information sheet.

"We need an emergency contact." I hand her the paper, ignoring the rush through my veins when her fingers brush mine.

She scrawls down a name and phone number.

"I didn't see the point; my parents live five hours away." She hands it back, clicking the pen shut.

Ignoring that comment, I open my schedule and she copies down the appointments I booked after Dane told me we hired someone.

Once we're done, I shove the book back into my desk. I have them saved in my computer, but I like to have a paper copy as well, just in case.

I walk her out, locking the door behind us. When she reaches her truck and trailer, she turns to face me, her lips pulled back in that same friendly but indifferent smile she's been wearing all day. It irritates me.

"Dane said you would show me where the apartment is." She adjusts the hem of her shirt, looking up at me with the first hint of apprehension I've seen since she walked in.

Of course, he did.

Sighing, I turn on the heel of my boot and gesture for Reese to follow me.

CHAPTER TWO

Reese

Ryan strides past me without a word and no attempt to hide his expression of annoyance. He could've saved himself the task had he shown me the apartment on the tour, but I'm positive he forgot that I was moving in.

My eyes drop to his ass as he takes long strides past Lia's clinic. He has a great ass, his Wrangler jeans accentuating how firm it is. I'm as ass kind of woman, hence why I've always been drawn to cowboys because they almost always have nice butts.

Flushing, I tear my eyes away. I shouldn't be checking out my boss. With the smirk on his face when I first walked in the door, I know he's probably a womanizer. I've seen that smirk before. I married a man with that same smirk and it landed me in a load of trouble.

As we approach the apartment, I can tell by the layer of sawdust on the ground that the door is a new addition. A covered stoop, which also looks new, spreads over the door to about six feet on each side and six feet out. On one side of the porch is a little bistro set that looks custom-made. I can picture myself reading outside with a steaming cup of tea, especially since it overlooks some of the horse pens and nothing beats sitting outside and watching horses just do their thing.

I have a feeling these features are modifications made in haste for me. It shows the wealth and staying power the Hyatt family has in this community, not that they flaunt it. I spent hours on the ranch website reading up on all the services they offer, including some of the pro bono work they do and other things they've contributed to the community. They're incredible and despite the less-than-enthusiastic welcome, I'm excited to be here.

"We added the door and locked the one that goes directly into the clinic. That way you won't disrupt Lia and you have some privacy." Ryan bends down and pulls a key out from under the mat, a twinge of excitement courses through me as he unlocks the door.

For the first time in seven years, I'm excited to kick my shoes off in my own home. Actually, if I'm being honest, I haven't felt that a space belonged to me for longer than that. I lost everything with the divorce, aside from my truck, trailer, and my horse, Sasha. My business suffered because our divorce took almost three years and Justin made sure to tie up as much of my time in litigation as he possibly could. By the time I signed the divorce papers, most of my clients had moved on to other farriers that didn't have a constantly changing schedule. The ones who stuck around eventually disappeared because of the drama Justin continued to try and inflict on my life.

I moved back in with my parents at twenty-seven to deal with everything. I almost gave up, but I'm no quitter and over the past several years I've tried to get my business up and running again. It's been tough, Justin is a big name in the rodeo circuit and he ran my name through the wringer after the separation and divorce.

That's the thing about abusers. Even after you've left and tried to cut them off, they still want that control over you and I just wanted him out of my life for good. At first, I thought I could help him work through his anger. Help him sort out whatever issue he had that led him to be the way he was. I went to a support group for people whose spouses have difficulty managing their anger. I went to therapy. I tried everything I could to provide a safe and supportive environment, encouraging him to seek help for whatever was going on. Until the emotional abuse became physical. Until the idea of ending my life to stop the pain started to become a plan instead of an idea.

I'm safe. I'm out of an abusive relationship, and I don't have to deal with people looking at me like I'm the one that messed everything up when they don't know anything about what happened. I've also promised myself not to enter in to a relationship with a cocksure guy ever again. I want someone sweet, steady, and kind.

Sighing, I think about how much I've lost. It didn't matter how hard I tried to build my business back up, I couldn't gain enough clients to stay afloat. That's when I realized I couldn't do this on my own. The community is too small for me to re-establish myself without someone backing me up. I knew I needed to have a good name associated with mine in order to stabilize my life and my career.

In an act of desperation, I hit the internet and scoured the forums for local farriers. When I saw the Hyatt's ad—by sheer luck—as I was scrolling through a search engine, it seemed like fate. I did a lot of research about the Hyatt family and their ranch, including the location, and it felt like the right fit.

There's something about the family-centered business that drew me to them and I decided to apply.

Honestly, I was a little shocked that Dane agreed to interview me, since a quick search of my name online would reveal the rumors that I haven't been able to shake. And in this day and age, I assumed employers researched their potential employees. That is until I met him. Dane was so kind, his questions insightful and focused. We went through the interview process, without any mention about my fall from grace, then he asked if I had any questions. Instead of beating around the bush, I went for transparency and opened up about the last several years, fully expecting him to dismiss me. Instead he reminded me that my experience and my references outweigh any backlash they may receive and as a family they would stand by me if needed. He offered me the position right after.

Walking in to the clinic and meeting Ryan, the eldest of the Hyatts, the presence he filled the room with was completely different than the one Dane presented. The smoldering look he greeted me with nearly stopped me in my tracks.—That sexy smile combined with a deep, resonate voice made my stomach flutter a little—and then I introduced myself. The room went from hot to cold with a suddenness that left me a little breathless.

His behavior after he found out I'm his employee is underwhelming. No different than every other cocky farrier I've met. I guess I should be thankful that it's not because I'm a woman that he dislikes me, or even my reputation in the business now that Justin has destroyed the name I was starting to build for myself, but simply that he doesn't want anyone in on his business. It's just too bad for him this job is too appealing to abandon it because of his shitty attitude. He's not the first jackass I've worked with, I know how to handle myself.

If I was the type to run scared, I would've hightailed it out of there at the look of complete and utter aggravation he gave me. Too bad for him I'm used to it, and I'm much too stubborn to cower, especially since I finally feel like I'm on the path to set my life right again. I'm not about to sacrifice myself and my well-being at the hands of a guy.

Not again.

I lost myself with my ex-husband, allowed him to knock me down way more than I thought I would tolerate, and it won't happen again. I'm not cold, I understand my ex has deep issues that need to be dealt with and those issues can change the core of who a person is, but I just couldn't do it anymore. I tried. I tried so hard to the point it's four years later and I'm just starting to recognize myself when I look in the mirror.

The lock clicks open, Ryan handing me the key before swinging the door open and holding it for me caused my brows to lift in surprise. Glancing up, I meet his dark gaze for a second, and maybe I'm imagining it, but I think I see a hint of vulnerability before the arrogant mask slides back into place.

As I pass, I try to ignore the warmth that floods my body when I accidentally brush against him, the scent of his masculine cologne heady. Stepping quickly to the side, I turn my gaze to the apartment. Dane warned me it was simple and small, but all I see is perfection and a second chance.

Slipping my shoes off, I tuck them to the side before moving into the center of the room, my eyes devouring my new space. The flooring is all tile; a color palate of sand, cream, and a warm toned gray. It's open concept, the kitchen and living space all one room. Small, but functional. Everything is designed to fit in the space. The furniture is rustic and quaint. I would be willing to bet it—and the little bistro set—was made by someone on the ranch.

The bedroom and bathroom are off to one side, again furnished in a simple, rustic style. There is a built-in wardrobe that takes up an entire wall in the space, more than enough room for my clothes. There is enough room around the bed for me to walk and nothing more, but it's perfect.

"There's no laundry here, you can come to the main house to wash your clothes, just coordinate with Lia what day works because she keeps track of the household schedule. It won't be long before she's over here introducing herself." Ryan's tone is gruff with a hint of affection when he speaks of his sister. His posture is awkward as he watches me move about the small space from where he still stands on the mat by the door.

"Sounds great." I'd agree to doing my laundry by hand in a washbasin at this point, anything to make this work.

He walks outside with a huff when I start opening cupboards and exploring more thoroughly. When I finally head back outside his head is bent over his phone, his thumbs flying over the keyboard. I can't imagine using his thumb in that way is recommended with his injury, but I'm almost positive he would still be working if it was up to him. He could probably do it too; the man exudes stubbornness.

As I stand on the porch of my new home, I take a deep breath. For the first time in so long, I feel like I can finally breathe again. Part of my salary includes living here rent free, something that will save my ass as I dig myself out of the debt I've racked up. Between the cost of therapy, my divorce lawyer, the divorce settlement, and trying to survive after the divorce was finally finalized, I'm in deep. This job could be considered a step down from owning my own business, but the security is worth it. The contract I signed gives me three months to show my worth, and I'm determined to demonstrate I'm an asset to their business and their ranch.

"All good?" he asks me, his voice a deep appealing rumble even with the grouchy undertone. I can tell by the way he's glancing at his phone that he just wants to get out of here.

"Yeah, I just need to unload my horse. Dane said there is a pen I can house her in—" I trail off, hoping he will direct me to which corral will be her new home.

He starts walking before I've finished speaking to the pen closest to the apartment. It's quite large, spanning over a small field and into the trees. Clean, bright boards are intermixed with some of the more weathered rails telling me it's been recently cleaned and fixed up. It contains an automatic waterer, a bale of hay in a hay net, and a shelter strategically positioned to block the wind. He opens the gate and waits for me, his booted foot tapping in the dirt, impatient even though I never asked him to stay.

I quickly pull my truck around, backing into the space close to the pen, and park. It's clear it's a parking pad and it's long enough to leave my trailer and my truck without them being in the way. Unlatching the back of the trailer, I open the stall Sasha is tied in and pull the lead rope loose before wrapping my arms around her neck.

"This is our fresh start, Sasha. I can feel it." Whispering into her mane, I breathe in the comforting horse smell before I let go so I can guide her off the trailer, enjoying the way Ryan's eyes get that glazed over look I always see when horse professionals set eyes on her.

Sasha is a registered Appaloosa. She's solid black except for her white hindquarters that are spotted with black. She is my heart and soul, the only thing I really fought for in my divorce. I sacrificed a lot to keep her and I would do it all over again.

Ryan doesn't say much as he watches me settle Sasha into her new home. I turn on the automatic waterer, watching it fill, before checking her over while she eats. Once I'm satisfied that she doesn't have any cuts or other injuries, I let her off her halter and close the pen.

"Do you have any heavy boxes you need help carrying

inside?" Ryan's voice is grudging, but his question hints at a kind guy beneath the gruff exterior. I've seen a few of these glimpses since I arrived, and it gives me hope because I already love it here, and I want to enjoy working for him. Maybe with a little time we can form a solid partnership, maybe even find a little comradery.

"Thank you, but everything I packed I can manage alone. A friend of mine will be dropping the rest of my stuff off in a couple of hours, she can help me if I need it," I say as I close the trailer.

"If you like, there's a spare tack locker in my shop. I need to make a key for you still, but you can keep stuff in there. The apartment doesn't have room for much more than the bare necessities." His lips have yet to revisit the smile that first greeted me, but I give him a wide smile at his gesture.

"That would be wonderful, thank you." I infuse every bit of gratefulness I can into my voice. Mom always used to say, "Kill em' with kindness." My dad always piped in with some inappropriate joke, but I'm determined to counter every hostile look or remark with a friendly one of my own.

He nods, his eyes scanning the small stack of boxes he can see, before turning without another word and walking away. I watch his departure, the way the muscles in his legs flex with each step, his biceps bulging as he pulls himself into his truck and as it disappears down the driveway.

Sighing, I watch the cloud of dust that he leaves in his tracks, before unhooking my trailer and getting in my truck to pull it forward. This job is going to be interesting if that attitude keeps up, but I think I can wear him down. I'm hoping the rest of the family is as kind and warm as Dane was.

Opening the other stall, I unload the few belongings I brought with me and haul them into the apartment. My sister is coming with her husband and their son with my desk and a few other necessities I didn't have the cash to buy. I'm lucky they're only about two hours away from me.

It doesn't take me long to unpack, I only had two suitcases of clothes and a few small boxes of personal items. Glancing at my phone, I see a new text from Michelle letting me know they're about half an hour away.

I'm sure she forced Jim to leave early to get here sooner. They have their shit together, I've never seen a more well-suited couple, but I always laugh at his bending to her incessant need to leave at least an hour early almost any time they go anywhere.

I pass the time by cataloguing everything in the apartment. There isn't much, it appears most of what used to be in here was cleared out. They probably assumed I had everything I would need for the household.

Glancing at the clock, I decide to head outside to pass the time until they arrive. Looking around, I notice a path. Meandering down the trail, I push through some overgrown bushes to uncover an old gardening shed. The brush around it is overrun, shrubs encroaching on its walls. The door is jammed shut, but a couple of yanks later and I'm peering into the cutest little hideout I've ever seen. Despite the obvious disuse, it's clear that at one time or another, this space was well-loved.

Before I have time to explore further, I hear tires on the road, so I push my way back through the brush to greet my sister and brother-in-law.

Jim parks in front of my truck. Michelle hops out and rushes around to me, leaving her door wide open. When she wraps me in her arms, the floral scent of her perfume envelops me, it smells like good memories and home.

"Wow. This is quite the setup, not what I was picturing at all. I suppose you're right, this is the right choice." She approves, keeping one arm wrapped around me while Jim unties the straps holding down my things.

When I told my parents I was moving five hours away from them, there was quite the uproar. I get it, the last seven years haven't been kind to me, and they don't even know the half of it. They don't know the extent of the mountain of debt looming over me. And despite everything, I never could bring myself to tell them about the emotional and physical abuse I endured, even Michelle doesn't know the full extent. She has no idea I'm drowning in debt either and I'm too ashamed to tell her. My father treats my mother like his treasure, he is the perfect role model of what a husband and father should be, yet somehow, I missed all the signs with Justin.

"Hey, Jim. Thanks for doing this." I grin at my brother-in-law, his face already red from the afternoon heat. My sister definitely got it right with him. He reminds me a lot of my father in the ways that count. Michelle and Sean come first, always. He is an equal partner in their relationship in every way. And he's really come through for me.

He smiles at me, his laugh lines even more pronounced. "Any time. You know that."

"Where's Sean?" I peek into the back of their truck, looking for my ten-year-old nephew.

"He was invited to a friend's birthday party." Michelle smiles apologetically before rolling her eyes. "He's at that age where he just wants to be around his friends at all times."

We unload the truck, the three of us making quick work of the boxes before Jim shoos us away while he puts together my desk.

I show Michelle the apartment and assure her I don't need help cleaning it or rearranging it. The woman loves to rearrange furniture, but my family has already done so much for me and I finally feel ready to tackle this on my own in my own way.

We're sitting outside on my little porch when she glances at me with a funny look on her face.

"What?" Narrowing my eyes, I watch as she shifts in her seat.

"We ran into Justin yesterday." She broaches the subject of my ex-husband cautiously. It's taken me a long time to get over how awful he was in the last two years of our three-year marriage and throughout the two and a half years it took to finalize our divorce. For a long time, I refused to say his name because all it did is fill me with shame, until I recognized I have nothing to be ashamed over.

"Yeah?" I'm curious, the only reason she would be bringing him up is if there was some juicy piece of gossip to share.

"He's hooked up with a barrel racer from Arizona. I guess he's moving down there." Her voice carries disdain for him, there's never been any love lost between them.

"I feel bad for her, I doubt she knows what she's getting into." Closing my eyes, I try to quench the guilt I feel that he's probably abusing another woman.

"He wanted to get your number, said he needed to talk to you." She scoffs. "I told him where to go and how to get there."

"After all this time he's still trying to hook his way back into my life." I can't mask my contempt for him.

Closing my eyes, I remember when I first met him. He was so charming, that boyish smile artfully designed to draw you in. A mask, a persona to hide the angry man seething beneath the surface.

She reaches out and squeezes my hand, holding it until I unclench my jaw and release the breath I'm holding. "Look, what you went through, I can't imagine how horrible it was.

Just remember he needs to live with his choices too and maybe one day he will get help."

"All done." Jim comes out, oblivious to the tense moment. "How did it go meeting your new boss?"

"It was fine." I lie, knowing if I tell him the truth he'll get protective and want to speak with Ryan. Besides, I can handle Ryan. He's nothing compared to the hell I've endured.

"Good." He wraps his arm around Michelle. "Babe, we gotta get going if we want to pick Sean up on time."

We say goodbye, Michelle squeezing me tightly with tears in her eyes.

"I love you, sis. Call if you need anything." She waits for my nod before leaving.

Locking the door behind them, I head into my room and lay down on my bed. The silence of the apartment is overwhelming. I can hear the whir of the fridge and when the air conditioning kicks in I practically jump out of my skin. I've never lived on my own. I went from my parents' house to a dorm to shared accommodations when I was apprenticing with Roy to living with Justin before moving back to my parents' house.

This is a brand new experience. It's scary, but the little flutter in my stomach is one of excitement. I can't wait to start this new journey. It's my time to finally reinvent myself and be the person I'd imagined.

CHAPTER THREE

Ryan

Flipping the lights in my shop, I prop the door open to allow a breeze to blow in. It's already a hot day and it's not even eight o'clock. Returning to my truck, I grab the new office chair I bought for Reese last night, and set it on the concrete floor before rolling it to the desk.

I hear her boots on the gravel before she's in the doorway. Her legs are clad in jeans, the smooth tips of her steel-toed boots peeking out from under the denim. She's wearing another plaid shirt, this time it's tucked loosely into her jeans. Grunting a greeting, I zone in on her smile as she says "good morning" in a raspy voice.

"I baked banana bread last night, I thought you might like some." She holds out the bread, wrapped in plastic wrap.

Staring at it, I try to ignore the rumble of my stomach as I drop my gaze to the calendar I've pulled out of the desk drawer.

"We have four clients today and a total of thirteen horses. I've scheduled them back to back, factoring in driving time. We should pack up and go." Snagging my phone from the top of the desk, I tuck it in my rear jean pocket and leave the shop, bypassing the banana bread. I don't want her baking me delicious goods. I don't want to like her. And I want to pretend that when she smiled at me, it didn't make my stomach react in that way that leads to nothing but trouble.

I hear her sigh as she moves about the shop gathering her tools and I try to ignore the strong physical reaction of my body to that sound. Hopping in my truck, I start it and crank the country station while I wait for her to load her tools and join me.

Reese opens the passenger door, pausing without getting inside. "Should you be driving with that?"

Her soft tone does nothing to dampen the rise of irritation.

"I'm not an invalid. I can drive with my cast. I'm still mobile, I just can't do physical labor. Lucky for you, because otherwise you wouldn't be here."

She nods, her cheeks flushing as she rushes to hop inside rather than delay us any longer.

Turning out of my client's driveway, I glance over at Reese warring with myself. She's gazing out the window, her fingers tapping on her knee as the trees blur by, her ponytail is loose, stray hair sticking straight out around her face. If I wasn't so annoyed, I'd think it was cute, but it's been a long effing day. Her first official day—and, well let's say I wasn't really impressed.

I promised Dane I would give her the full three months of

her contract, give her a fair opportunity. After the fiasco today turned into, I regret that agreement.

Returning my focus to the road, I work my jaw as I remind myself to call Roy again. He didn't return my call last night, and I want his input on Reese as a farrier. Scratch that, I want him to tell me that Dane made a huge mistake in hiring her and that we should let her go. I was itching the entire time she worked today, the urge to take over so strong I had to walk to my truck and pretend to take a call.

"I can see you stewing over there, why don't you tell me what you're thinking. Perhaps provide me with some *constructive* feedback, so that way I know what I can improve." She angles her body toward me, her eyes full of trepidation, but her voice firm and determined.

"We were an hour too long with the first three appointments. You let the owners distract you with chit chat, so each horse took longer than necessary." I can't disguise the frustration in my voice. Each word is forced out from my clenched jaw.

She nods, absorbing my criticism in silence rather than arguing with me like I expected. She seems to surprise me at every turn, not reacting or behaving in the way I expect.

"Due to the amount of time each horse took, I had to reschedule our final appointment of the day. Your quality of work was good, but you need to do better while going faster. You have ten years of experience, those horses stood perfectly and only needed a trim. They shouldn't take more than ten minutes each." Pausing, I focus on passing a tractor. She continues to watch me, meeting my gaze when I glance at her.

"The client I had to reschedule has been with me for three years, in that time I've never missed an appointment. He took the afternoon off work to be there and have his horse ready for us. He was understandably put out, he doesn't get paid for missed work, and I couldn't fit him in until next week, a week too long for his horse. You need to be able to meet the expectations of my clients, you're representing me, my family, and our ranch. The work you do, your presentation to clients, impacts the reputation my family has been building since my parents started the business thirty years ago." My voice is loud in the small cab of my truck, drowning out the quiet music we were listening to.

She nods. "I will do better tomorrow." Her voice is quiet, accepting before she turns her head to gaze out the window.

As we near the ranch, I glance at her again, her face still directed away from me. She's sitting tall in her seat, it looks incredibly uncomfortable and when I continue to stare I notice a slight quiver to her chin, it's subtle but I don't miss it. Focusing back on the road, I bite back the feeling of guilt that surfaces. I'm being intentionally hard on her, I know that. And, truth be told, we probably could have made it to Hunter's house, but I just couldn't handle watching her anymore. I'm more upset with myself and the situation I'm in than I am with Reese.

It was difficult seeing my clients transition to another farrier without a second thought, I forced myself to stay quiet on the sidelines and it irked me. They smiled and joked with her as she worked, an air of confidence surrounding her that was undeniably appealing.

To top it off, I also got to stare at her perfect ass the entire time she was bent over trimming. The way her cheeks would flush with the exertion was adorable and the fact that I was staring at her more than focusing on what she was doing set me on edge.

There's just something about her that's kept her at the forefront of my thoughts since she walked in the door and it's made me feel ill at ease all day. That draw from yesterday is still there and I don't understand or like it.

It makes it worse that she's a nice person who I actually like, and I don't want to like her, for more reasons than one.

Grudgingly, I admit to myself that my clients seemed to appreciate how friendly she is. If I'm being completely honest with myself, I've been so busy the last year that I realize I've lost sight of the personal side to the business, something Reese seems to have a knack for, she even managed to make old Gunderson smile. I've never seen him smile. And he called her darlin' in an affectionate tone before he turned those shrewd eyes on me.

On the other hand, I started her off with the casual horse owners, not the competitive ones, and they tend to be easier going about things.

We finish the drive back to the shop in silence. Reese glances over at me as we park, her eyes conveying how upset she is, even as she gives me a small smile. It makes me feel like complete shit. I should apologize for being so harsh, but I can't seem to form the words. She deserves some positive feedback, but instead of manning up, I keep my mouth shut until she turns to exit the truck.

Her auburn hair is tied back, showing off her defined cheekbones. She's a beautiful woman, one I would absolutely be inviting into my bed if circumstances were different. I also saw a kind heart today, making me feel even worse about how hard I was on her.

It's not her fault I didn't want help or that I'm unhappy not being able to do the things I normally enjoy doing. This broken arm is making me a miserable son of a bitch.

Hopping out, I start to try to unload my truck, but Reese moves into my path. "I've got this."

She grabs her tools, not even bothering to make multiple

trips. The muscles in her arms hold the weight effortlessly, the definition both strong and feminine.

As I watch her, the reason she sets me on guard hits me like a freight train. If I was in the market for something serious, she would be my ideal woman. She's smart, not afraid to work hard, a country woman to the core, and stunningly beautiful. My body is drawn to her, and today my mind was too as I listened to her interact with my—our—clients. It's easier to keep her at a distance than risk developing more than amicable feelings, so my defense mechanism kicked into high gear.

I haven't felt this way since Cece, who was using me to elevate herself in the horse world. Once she got to the position she wanted she dropped me like a bad habit and happily ran off and married some exec, leaving me with an unworn engagement ring and a broken heart.

I told myself after that fiasco I wouldn't put myself in a position to be hurt again, and I haven't. Nothing like having your heart ripped out of your chest by your first love. Being taken advantage of, used, and then dropped like you don't matter, it's a guaranteed way to shut down someone's heart and my heart has been closed off for the last five years.

Just thinking about the vulnerability one has to open themselves to in order to be in a relationship makes my skin crawl with discomfort.

The worst part is running into her occasionally, the sickly sweet smile she turns in my direction is so fake. I can't believe I was ever gullible enough to fall for her lies.

The last time I ran into her, she tried to get me to go to her hotel room for "old times sake." She didn't take too kindly to me laughing in her face and calling her an adulterous bitch. Now she avoids me like the plague.

My skin feels prickly as I think about her, so I focus back on the woman I'm stuck with every day for the next three months.

She's fixed her ponytail, the luscious auburn locks swinging back and forth as she walks toward my shop.

Reese has the potential to break the casing I've stored my heart in. Somehow, I need to make it through the three months, and hopefully send her on her way with a recommendation and my sanity intact.

The door is unlocked and when I step inside I see Dane sitting in my chair, his feet propped on my desk. His eyes are perceptive when he watches Reese walk in, the obvious downward tilt to her lips. His narrowed gaze meets mine.

"How'd it go?" He turns his attention to Reese, clearly not caring what I have to say.

The smile she bestows on him is brilliant. "It was good. I was a little slower than would've been ideal, but I'll do better tomorrow."

Dane looks between us, taking in my scowl and responding with a glare of his own as Reese meanders over to the side of the shop.

She's silent as she drops everything on the counter, pulling out her tools. She cleans and sharpens each one before putting them away in her cabinet. She's quiet, unlike when she was interacting with clients. Today is only the first day, but I'm positive the only reason she's not chattier is because of my attitude. I don't usually like a lot of conversation when I'm working, but I feel the absence of her voice straight in my chest.

Dane looks about ready to blow a gasket when his phone rings. He glances at the screen, swiping his finger to answer and leaves the shop, but not before he gives me a look that tells me he will be talking to me later.

When Reese is done with her tools, she turns to face me. Her expression is carefully schooled into what I've dubbed her "professional face."

I can't help myself, seeing the smile she bestowed on Dane got my back up, I hated it. "He's unavailable, just so you know. And he's not about to risk everything he has with Emma, no matter how pretty you smile at him."

As soon as the words leave my mouth I feel sick.

Her face pales, her eyes flashing, and when she speaks her tone is low and hard. "Let me set the record straight. I smile at everyone, it doesn't mean I'm being suggestive or flirtatious. I'm not here to hook up with anyone, I'm here to do my job and that's it."

Heady silence fills the room as we wait the other out.

Finally, her shoulders fall as she looks away.

"Anything left to do today?" Her soft voice carries a heaviness that wasn't there earlier, all fight gone. The weight of my words has settled over her and a part of me hates myself for putting it there.

"If you want to head out for the day, I can do the paperwork." I drop down into my chair, pull my laptop out of its drawer and boot it up.

"No, I should learn what to do." Her voice is quiet as she comes over, pausing momentarily at the brand new chair waiting for her before she drops down and inches closer to me.

She smells like coconut and a hint of lime; her scent has been following me around all day. I love coconut, it reminds me of summer days in simpler times. She's unintentionally torturing me as she leans in to look at my computer screen.

I go over the billing and how I've organized each client file. She's quiet except to ask questions. By the time we've sent invoices to the clients we saw today along with a reminder for the next appointment, Reese has demonstrated that she's not only talented with the animals and clients, but also the business side of the job.

We finish up quickly, Reese standing as soon as the final

invoice is sent. I tuck my laptop away, watching as she heads for the door with a quiet "goodbye."

As her hand falls to the knob, I stand, my chair scraping back loudly in the silent room. "You did a good job with the Hershmann's herd today. Some of them can be a little persnickety and you nipped it all right in the bud."

She gives me a small smile, her cheeks flushing. "Thank you." Her tone is full of gratitude, and as she walks out the door, her shoulders are more relaxed.

My phone rings just as I'm locking up. Glancing down at the screen, I smile when I see Roy's name.

"Hey, old man! I thought I was going to have to hunt you down. How're the trainees you got going? Any good?" I smile as I walk toward my house. The workers are gone for the day, so I'm going to sneak around and make sure everything is correct. Technically, I'm "banned" from the construction site, but I figure it's my damn house and I need to be sure they're not messing anything up.

"Too early to tell. Not all of them can have the raw talent you did. I've had many students and only a handful are naturals. The others, well, it's all learned. They don't have that instinct." Roy's gruff voice is low and I'm positive it gets deeper every time we talk. Likely due to the pack of cigarettes he smokes a day.

Tsking when he coughs, I lightly scold, "I thought you were quitting."

He grunts. "I'm too set in my ways. Now, you sounded upset in your message. What's going on?"

"Long story short, I got kicked and fractured my arm. Dane hired someone on a three-month contract that stipulates there is the possibility for a permanent position as my employee. There's just something off about her story and I understand she apprenticed with you. Her name is—"

"Reese McMillan. I knew Dane hired her, he called me for a reference." Roy chuckles, and it's impossible to miss the affection in the sound. I know just by that laugh he's not going to tell me what I was hoping. "That girl has more talent in her pinky than ninety percent of the people I've ever trained. You and her both have a natural talent for this work and the fact that she wants to work for you full-time, well, that's a blessing."

Stopping in front of my house, I stare at it numbly.

"I can tell that's not what you want to hear, but I'm going to give you some advice and you need to listen. You hang on to her. You work through your hang-ups, and you appreciate the fact that her tool of an ex-husband made it necessary for her to go in this direction." He pauses, his voice heavy with disappointment. "I never took you to be sexist."

"Gender has nothing to do with it." My voice is sullen, the words mumbled. "It's pure stubbornness combined with a need for control."

"Plus she's an attractive woman and that Cece did a number on you. Son, not every woman gets a kick out of playing with people's feelings for their own selfish desires. Reese is a mature woman who ain't got time for nonsense. She was broken-hearted after her divorce and that schmuck took everything from her except her horse, the trailer, and the clothes on her back. You ain't got nothin' to worry about." His no-nonsense demeanor tells me everything I'd already figured out but was too stubborn to admit.

I knew from the moment she got a smile out of Gunderson that she's an asset to the ranch. He's one of my most critical clients. Once a farrier himself, he's sharp as a whip and will critique you without pause. I need to get my head out of my ass, it's just tough to admit that to myself. However, that doesn't mean I can't work her hard and push her to do better, because if what he says is true, she didn't put her best foot forward today and I need her to be at her best always.

After we hang up, I find the new information I've learned about Reese stuck in my head as I wander around my house, especially the fact that she's divorced. She's lived a different path than I have, and I can see how her perspective on the world may differ from mine.

We've both been hurt, and she said today she's not here for anything other than to work, maybe I can keep my distance but utilize the extra help the way my family needs me to do.

Sighing, I focus on inspecting the progress on my house and find it to my satisfaction. At the rate they're going, we should be at lock-up before the snow flies, which means if Reese is still here by the time I move in early next year, we're going to be isolated neighbors.

I need to get over my attraction to Reese. I need to keep my head on straight. She's someone I will see everyday, someone who could become a permanent member of the ranch, and therefore an added member to our family. I need to be sure to treat her like I would Emma or Nella.

CHAPTER FOUR

Reese

Sitting at the quaint bistro set occupying my little porch, I pull my boots on before leaning back and taking a long sip of my coffee. The sigh that escapes is one of pure bliss. The warm morning air has that summer smell I can't get enough of, like hot dirt and flowers, and it's almost serene enough to make me forget how tired I am. Sleep was elusive, all I could think about was Ryan and his obvious hope that I fail. I couldn't even get him to smile over banana bread. Then all day I could hear him sighing and grunting before reaming me out in the truck.

What he doesn't realize is that his attempts to freeze me out and get me to quit are futile. I refuse to move back in with my parents. I'm thirty-four, and he's not the first asshole who hasn't wanted to work with me.

The heaviness in my heart contradicts the strength of my thoughts. I want him to like me. I want to have a good working relationship—not a hostile working environment—while I get back on my feet again. A good chunk of my twenties was spent walking on eggshells, I don't want that again. This job is supposed to lead me to my forever.

The miniscule ray of light, the thing that gives me courage, is the compliment he gave me at the end of the day. It's that little shred of hope that I'm going to cling to as we work today.

On the bright side, I'm isolated from the family except for when I need to do laundry, so if he doesn't warm up to me I don't need to see him after work too. Thinking about laundry reminds me I have to contact Lia to arrange a day or two I can go to the main house and use their machines. I'm hoping she is friendly like Dane, I could use the company of friends.

The timer beeps on my phone, alerting me it's day two of working for Ryan. We have one client today, but he's two hours away and has thirty horses. It won't be the first time I've had a day like this, but it's been a long time. Ryan is clearly not making any accommodations to ease me in, which I must admit I appreciate.

In my experience, men either try to coddle me, sleep with me, or are completely rude and dismissive. Ryan is a little of the latter, but he did manage to give me a couple compliments yesterday and they didn't even sound forced. Granted, the first one seemed like it wasn't intentional, but I'll take it.

Setting my cup on the small table just inside the door, I lock up and make the short walk to the shop. My boots crunch on the gravel, loud in the quiet of the early morning. The sound of Ryan's voice carries out the open shop door.

I peer inside, his back is to the door as he talks on the phone in a low voice. When he laughs, tingles run down my spine. It's deep, rumbly, and I could listen to that sound all day.

Shivering, I watch this different side to him. The relaxed unguarded version. The man I see before me is the man I suspect he is on a day to day basis. He laughs again, the sound pleasant.

"You're not going to convince her otherwise. Alex, she's determined to see the show season through. She has her final one the first weekend in September, and there is no way you're convincing her otherwise. She's going, and you just need to be okay with it." When he's not scowling and grumpy, his voice has a nice timbre to it. He has the kind of voice you can imagine saying dirty things, in just the right way. Scoffing at myself, I shake off the thought, but another takes its place.

An ache blooms in my chest. When I first met Justin, he was so charming and his voice was one of the things that drew me in. I knew he had a reputation for being a flirt and for not wanting to settle down, but his charm sucked me in and I was helpless against it.

This side of Ryan kind of reminds me of the Justin I fell in love with. The easy laugh, the teasing nature. There was so much to *like* about Justin and he made me feel cherished at first. A feeling I miss with an intensity as I listen in, from the outside.

Don't get me wrong, looking back the warning signals of Justin's abusive nature were there. A moodiness and unpre-dictability I equated to the stress of shows. We were already married the first time Justin told me I was worthless. I made an excuse for him, thinking it was a one-time thing. The weeks following, he was even more intensely affectionate, and I craved his undivided attention. He exuded charm and he was able to convince me not to be worried.

It's apparent Ryan has the charm and swagger, the draw to him that Justin did, but without the extraneous issues, because despite the scowl on his face he didn't say anything inappro-priate or degrading yesterday. Well, that's not entirely true, but I could see his sharp remark about me trying something with

Dane came from somewhere internal. I don't know him well enough to assess what kind of baggage he's carrying, but I'm guessing that comment gives a hint.

Shaking my head, I close the door so Ryan knows I'm here. I'm ten years older and ten years wiser than I was when I met Justin. Our relationship was a whirlwind, we were married in six months, it took less than a year for his abusive nature to wreak havoc on our life. There is no sense on dwelling on the past and what I once thought was my great love, it's over. I just need to get my life together and I'm going to do it on my own, find my new forever.

"I gotta go. Deep breaths, dude. Lia is a pro. Ollie is steady. That baby is going to be fine and so is she." Ryan turns as he wraps up his conversation. A genuine smile is on his face and it damn near knocks the wind out of me. It's different than the smile he first gave me yesterday, the one filled with innuendo, this one radiates affection for his family. As soon as he hangs up, the smile is gone and I miss it immediately.

"We better get on the road. Do you have your tools ready?" His voice is gruffer than when he was talking on the phone, but it still impacts me. My heart is caught in the memory of what I thought I had and the similarities in the two men.

Justin was the master of the honeymoon period, so much so that I continued to make excuses until he hit me for the first time. Part of the reason I chose to apply here is because the chances of my heart getting involved is slim. I can't let my heart get involved, because I don't trust it to know what's good for it. And the attraction for Ryan that I feel pulsing through my body is definitely not good for me.

He cocks an eyebrow when I just stand there and stare at him.

Rolling my shoulders, I rush to my cabinet and grab my stuff.

"I'm ready."

We're twenty minutes into our drive and Ryan has spoken less than ten words. I counted. I like to think I'm thick-skinned, and when it comes to work I definitely am, but this situation is a little different. I'll be spending five days a week with Ryan in some capacity, not to mention the possibility of running into him in our off time, and I want to find some common ground. Desperately.

"So, that's quite the house going up by the clinic. Who's building it?" I don't fake the enthusiasm in my voice, the house is stunning. It's basically my dream house, a combination of Victorian and country rustic design. I may have wandered over there last night to dream and wish.

"It's a local builder, Douglas Brothers Custom Homes." His voice is missing the warm tone it held when he was on the phone earlier, but it's also missing the irritation it usually holds when we talk. That's gotta be a win.

"That's cool. I actually meant which one of you is building." I smile, trying not to sound exasperated. Clearly, I meant which sibling is building the house.

"That would be me." He flicks on his turn signal and slows down as we reach a gravel road.

"When do you get to move in?" He can try to give as little as he wants, but I'm determined. It didn't escape my notice that the banana bread was gone from his desk this morning.

"Probably March, depending on the weather and scheduling the trades." He glances over at me. "They're pretty close to lockup and the builder always has the next stuff booked and ready to go."

"That's good, makes it a little less stressful. It's a beautiful home." I turn from his gaze, glancing out the window as we pass a golden field of canola.

"Thanks, I designed it myself." This time when he speaks, his voice is full of pride instead of annoyance, but instead of carrying on the conversation he falls silent once again.

Trying to hold a conversation with him is harder than trying to answer the dentist's questions with their hands in your mouth. Irritation makes my next words a little snarkier than I intend them. "I've never built a house, but I used to doodle on my graph paper in school. Dream up designs for houses and barns. Imagine what my property would eventually look like. It seems like a far-off dream now, but it used to keep me busy when I was bored."

There is a pause, Ryan's Adam's apple bobs as he swallows and I think he's just going to ignore me. But then he asks, "Did you have a favorite that you designed?"

"I did. It was country meets Victorian, not dissimilar to yours in a lot of ways. I've always wanted a house with a functional attic. My dream barn is basically the one your shop is attached to. Not too big, but functional and multi-purpose." I flush at the wistfulness in my tone, glancing at Ryan out of the corner of my eye.

He's staring straight ahead at the road, we're only halfway through our drive so I'm assuming the intensity of his focus is partially to do with me being in the vehicle. His fingers tap on the steering wheel, I hadn't paid much attention to his hands, but the motion draws my eyes. His hands are large, those fingers long and capable looking. Calluses demonstrate how hardworking he is, despite not being able to utilize an entire arm. There's something tremendously attractive about a man who works with his hands.

Dropping my gaze, I try to pretend my cheeks aren't

flushed and that there isn't a throbbing need building as I imagine what those fingers could do.

"You know, one of the perks of working on the ranch is that you can use the facilities. Don't feel like you need to ask to use the pool or arena. The only private one is the barn and arena next to the main house, and that's mostly because Lia is prepping for her shows." His voice is casual, seemingly unaware of how generous that allowance is. "Also included in your salary is access to Lia's services. Free of charge."

"Oh, wow. Really? Sasha's been a little tight and it's beyond my basic knowledge of equine massage." I'm surprised that they would offer that, and even more surprised that Dane didn't tell me when we were negotiating my contract.

"I noticed she was tight on the left hip, that's why I mentioned it." Ryan's tone shifts again. It's difficult to pinpoint what's going on in his head, but he doesn't say anything else.

We made a little progress today, so I let it go and tell myself to work at it a little every day.

Shifting in my seat, I glance at the time. We've been driving for a little over an hour. My phone rings, startling us both in the quiet of the truck.

Glancing at the screen, I answer when I see it's Michelle. "Hey, Mimi."

She chuckles at the nickname. When I was little I couldn't pronounce her name properly and the nickname stuck. "How's it going? How was your first day?"

I try to discreetly turn down the volume when Ryan glances my way, but it's near impossible to make it so he can't hear her while I still can. "It was good. I wasn't my fastest, but I'm working on it."

Michelle sees through my casual tone. "Reese, please tell me they're treating you right."

Angling my body away from Ryan, I pray my cheeks aren't

too red. "Of course. I'm just out of practice aside from Sasha and the Melner's horses. You don't maintain the same speed when you only do six horses every six weeks."

The "thanks, Justin" is silent, but I know Michelle picks up on my bitterness.

"I suppose. I'm sure your awesomeness isn't escaping them." She pauses to answer Jim before asking, "Have you talked to Mom and Dad?"

"Just a few texts." We've always been a close family, I know it's tough for them to have me so far away.

"And did you call Justin?" This time her question is cautious. I don't see why she's asking, she already knows the answer. Maybe she's making sure I'm not being sucked in, I may have given in to his "requests" to talk to me early on in our separation, so I understand her concern, but I haven't spoken with him outside of a courtroom in over five years.

"No, Michelle. Why would I call my ex-husband? The man who destroyed my reputation, pawned everything I ever had of value to stifle me financially, land me in a mountain of debt by dragging out divorce proceedings, and threatened to steal my horse? On top of all that, don't forget about the emotional and physical abuse I suffered and the turmoil I experienced when he swung to the opposite end of the spectrum and told me he would get help. Yeah, I'll call him when hell freezes over." My voice gets higher and higher as I talk, all professionalism out the window. "You know what, I have to trim thirty horses today, I can't deal with this and maintain my composure."

"I'm sorry, Reese. I just wanted to make sure." She pauses, thinking over her next words. "I know how lonely you've been."

Sagging lower into my seat, I bite back tears. "I don't care how lonely I am, I made myself a promise after the last time and I intend to keep it."

Hanging up, I lean down and root around in my purse. Finding the gummy bears I have stashed in there, I grab a red one and pop it in my mouth.

Closing my eyes so I can pretend Ryan isn't shooting me looks, I just keep eating the candy. My heart settles into its normal rhythm and I hold up the bag. "Gummy bear?"

There's a heavy pause, and then the pressure of his fingers against my palm as he takes some. In silence, we share the gummy bears until they're gone and I finally open my eyes.

"I'm really sorry about that, I shouldn't have lost my cool." My voice is sullen. He already doesn't want me here, and now I'm bringing drama into his life.

"I'm sure she was just looking out for you, but I understand how frustrating family can be when they think they know what's best for you." His voice is gentle, his expression soft as our eyes meet.

Before I can say anything, he's turning into a driveway and the moment is over.

"We have four hours to get through thirty horses. I trust that there's enough time?" He opens the door, his tone back to its usual coolness.

I quickly do the math.

"Eight minutes a horse. Sure, why not?" I hop down, my voice full of false bravado. Eight minutes a horse, I recalculate and sure enough, I'm not wrong. Swallowing hard, I grab my tools, meet the client and dive right in.

I bust my ass, working my way through each horse as quickly as I can while maintaining a quality level of work. My only saving grace is that Ryan has been working with these horses for close to a year and their feet aren't in bad shape, combining that with the fact that the owner isn't chatty so I don't feel guilty keeping my head down and working as fast as possible.

By the time I'm done, I worked for four and a half hours. Thirty minutes longer than planned.

As the owner, Allen, lets the last horse loose into their corral, I gather my tools and load the truck. Ryan leans against the passenger side, watching as I close the tailgate and sit on the bumper.

Allen walks up, a wide grin on his face. "It's a busy day, but we appreciate that you're willing to work with all of them." Allen reaches out to shake my hand, not caring that it's filthy and raw. "It was good to meet you. I suppose we'll be seeing you in eight weeks."

"You too."

We say goodbye, Ryan hopping in the truck as Allen opens the passenger side door for me. My feet are killing me as I drag myself after him and haul myself in. We exchange another goodbye before Allen closes the door and Ryan starts the truck.

He pulls out of the yard without saying anything. The energy is different than it was yesterday, but I'm still on edge. I went over his time by quite a bit. There has to be some comment stewing in that head of his.

"Okay, I can't take this. I went over the time by thirty minutes. I'm sorry, I really tried, but I didn't want to do a mediocre job." The words rush out, my fingers tapping on my knee.

Instead of getting all growly, he smirks, confusing the hell out of me. "What?" I drag the word out, my heart beating a little faster.

"It's fine, he expects it to take five hours. You did well." He grins as my jaw drops.

I don't even have a response. He told me I had less time than I actually did? Who does that? I'm torn between being pissed off at him and impressed that I beat his time by thirty minutes.

"I wanted to see what you could do with a little push." He shrugs, uncaring that I worked myself to the brink of exhaustion. "If it helps, I'm impressed."

My mouth opens and closes as I process this. At least he's happy, but still, my body hurts and my hands feel swollen. There are cuts marring them, and when I attempt to make a fist one splits open. Having that extra thirty minutes would've meant saving my body a little bit of pain.

Taking a deep breath, I turn to look out the window as I try to formulate some sort of coherent response. My eyes are heavy, so I close them to help me think better. Except, I'm so tired I feel myself start to drift off and I can't fight it.

CHAPTER FIVE

Ryan

Reese shifts in her seat with a soft moan. She looks incredibly uncomfortable with her chin resting on her chest and her head angled slightly to one side, but her face is peaceful and unmarred with the frustration she was clearly feeling before she passed out.

I know it was unfair to give her a shorter timeframe, but I wanted to see what she was capable of—and I'm impressed. I still need time to adjust to the idea of someone else having a hand in my business, but I can admit that maybe I was wrong to fight it so much.

Her being here, I know it will be good for the ranch even if it still unsettles me and her work improved drastically from yesterday. Although, in all fairness, yesterday's work was better than most farriers I've encountered and she's out of practice. Maybe it's possible that Roy's glowing recommendation combined with the realization I need to make the best of this situation helped clear the angry haze I've been living in. It feels good to not have that simmering frustration lingering constantly. My neck and shoulders have never been so tense.

Turning up the volume on the radio, I tap my fingers to the beat as I drive. A song mentions something about an ex-husband and I'm reminded of all the things Reese was saying about her ex to her sister.

Just hearing her talk about what he put her through makes me grip my steering wheel so tight, my knuckles turn white. I don't even realize I'm clenching the fist of my bad arm until it starts to ache something fierce.

The idea that she lived in an abusive relationship, that someone was capable of being abusive to her when she's clearly a kind-hearted soul, it makes me want to drive to wherever her lowlife ex is hiding and smack him around a little bit. It also makes me feel like shit for the way I've been treating her. My momma raised me better than that and I can just imagine the look on her face if she knew.

The fierce need to protect Reese rolls through me. Flexing my fingers, I remind myself that she's not my concern in that regard. She's my employee and will never be anything more. I need to lock this ache away, reserve it for Lia and Emma. For my family and the ranch.

Yet, the look on her face when I mentioned Lia working on Sasha for free, it was the look of someone who hasn't experienced a lot of compassion.

My chest constricts a little. She's had a rough go of it and I've really only made things worse, yet the not so funny thing is, she probably doesn't notice a huge difference from her past experiences and that just makes me feel like an even bigger jerk. If someone treated Lia or Emma that way—well, there would be hell to pay.

Thinking about that, I glance over at her before dialling Lia.

"Hey, big bro. How was Allen?" Lia's cheery voice is loud over the Bluetooth, so I turn it down and check to make sure Reese is still sleeping.

"Fine. We're on our way back now, Reese fell asleep. I wish that man lived closer, so I could split the herd into two days." My voice is wry. I wouldn't normally take on so many horses so far away, but Allen is a friend of my parents and his previous farrier made a mess of his herd. They're finally getting to the point where their growth is healthy, and it's taken close to two years.

"Anyway, what's up? You're not a phone person, so you're not calling just for idle chit chat." I hear Alex in the background, yelling that he will take the saddle from Lia and I realize I caught her on the tail end of practicing.

"You're going to give that man a heart attack," I chastise fondly before getting to the reason for my call. "Anyway, Reese has a horse, you've probably seen her."

"The gorgeous Appaloosa? Yeah, what about her?" I can hear the appreciation in Lia's voice and chuckle.

"Well, I noticed that she's a little stiff on the left side." Glancing over at Reese, I check to make sure she's still sound asleep. "And I kind of told her that part of her salary is free treatments from you. Obviously, I will pay you, but Reese doesn't have a lot of money and I think she would look at it like taking charity and I don't want her to refuse. So, just don't mention it to her. Okay?"

I suspected her financial situation was dire when I saw how worn her boots were. After overhearing her conversation with her sister, I know it's worse than I thought.

"Okay. I won't say a thing. I was going to go over and introduce myself tomorrow anyway, so I can take a closer look." I can hear the smile in her voice, a hint of smugness.

"Drop the tone, I'm just being nice because I care about the horse," I bite out, grumbling when Lia laughs at me.

I hang up, not wanting to indulge my sister any further into whatever idea she may have. My family doesn't know what happened with Cece, I was too damn embarrassed at the type of woman she turned out to be. Not that they really knew her, it should've been my first warning sign, she never had any interest in spending time with or getting to know my family.

What Reese went through is so much worse. I can't even imagine how someone who lived through that could open themselves up to someone again. It would take an immense amount of courage. Or stupidity. I'm not quite certain.

By the time I pull up to the shop, Reese is stirring. She sits up, blinking adorably as she takes in the fact she slept almost the entire way home.

"Wow, I really crashed." She's still half-asleep, so her usual guardedness is missing. "It's been a while since I've trimmed that many horses in a day. I think the last time was when I circulated the Canadian Finals Rodeo."

She opens her door, sliding out of the cab without waiting for a response from me. Before I can attempt to help her, she's already lugging her gear into the shop, the door shutting behind her.

I haven't done any research on Reese, or her past career, but little things here and there tell me that she used to have quite the name for herself, it's a wonder I've never heard of her before. I should ask her, but instead I decide to do a little employee recon this evening.

Leaving my truck running, I lock the shop up after she comes back out looking for me.

"We'll do the invoice tomorrow. Go relax." I give her a real smile for the first time since she walked in my door Sunday and introduced herself. "Lia will be swinging by sometime tomorrow to meet you, coordinate laundry, and book Sasha."

Reese returns my smile with a genuine one of her own and it makes her even more beautiful. The stress she carries with her disappears, and all I see is a talented and sexy woman who could easily be the second person to break my heart if I was willing to open myself up to her.

Dinner is already on the table when I walk in the door, Lia just setting down the last dish. My stomach growls. She inherited her amazing cooking skills from our mother, something that bypassed me.

"Emma and Dane are coming over. Just a warning since I know you've been avoiding him." Lia gives me a pointed look as she goes to the fridge and grabs a pitcher of iced tea. "I love knowing I'm more mature than my big brother."

Before I can respond, Alex saunters in and heads straight for my sister. His one hand rests on her belly as he leans in for a kiss. It's nauseating.

"You two are disgustingly happy." My voice is gentle, teasing. I'm so thrilled my siblings are happy, but it means the pressure is on me to settle down. Mom's already asked me why I'm building such a big house if I plan on enjoying it alone.

Ouch, Mom.

The door to the kitchen swings open, Dane and Emma laughing together as they walk in. Dane's eyes narrow when we lock gazes, softening only when Emma elbows him.

"You've been quiet this week," Emma chastises. "How's it going with Reese?"

I open my mouth to reply, but Lia cuts me off. "He thinks she's sexy."

"Dude, please tell me you're not trying to pick up Reese." Dane's exasperated tone grinds on my nerves.

"No, I'm not. I noticed something, and I attempted to do something nice. My mistake." I practically growl out the words, glaring at Lia.

"Oh. Well, I do hope you're trying to have a decent working relationship, but she's your employee. Nothing more."

"Right, I forgot. Me man. Me no able to control urges. Me pee in woods and bang woman over head with club." I add in some ape sounds for good measure, taking the steaming plate Alex hands me while rolling my eyes at Dane. Every woman who's ever been in my bed has chosen to be there. Every. Single. One. That's not about to change.

Lia and Emma cover their mouths giggling as Dane sighs and rolls his eyes.

"Whatever, as long as you're giving her a chance to show how qualified she is. Roy only had good things to say about her." Dane points at me with his fork as he talks, before taking a bite.

"I know. I called him." I know my family means well, but I'm about ready to pull the eldest sibling card.

Four skeptical faces stare at me, so I set my fork down and sigh. This is getting exhausting, but clearly they're not going to let my behavior slide anymore. Not that they should, I deserve it.

"I know I haven't been the easiest to get on board with this, you need to understand how difficult it is for me to feel completely useless. Not only to my clients, but to our business and all of you too. We're only a couple days in, she's still on probation in my mind, and I'm not going to sugar-coat any concerns I have." Dane starts to speak, but I hold my hand up. "That being said, I can see the benefit in expanding my side of the business. I will try harder to be a more pleasant employer and have a better attitude about this."

They finally lay off and we manage to have a pleasant dinner together. Hopefully this ends the strain we've been feeling, I hate being at odds with my family. We've always been close, never experiencing any detrimental sibling rivalries. We knew from a young age we wanted to continue to grow the family ranch once our parents retired, work together to do something we each loved. Having this distance from them, even for the short amount of time, has been weighing heavy on my mind.

We finish up, but instead of joining them in the living room to watch a movie, I head to my room and pull out my tablet. What I overheard when Reese was talking to her sister made me curious, so I search her name.

I'm inundated with social media posts talking about her fall from grace. How she's abandoning one of the community's most beloved, breaking his heart because she thinks she too good for a cowboy. How she's lying about her credentials. Post after post, comment after comment of people telling other people not to use her.

It's interesting, because as I dig deeper, I notice the opposite. People raving about her quality of work and how much of an asset she is to their team of horse care professionals.

Throughout my entire search, there's nothing mentioning Justin's abusive nature or anything like that. And as I explore, there is nothing from Reese about the matter. Her social media is all open for public viewing, and every post is positive, which says a lot about her character.

Setting my tablet onto my nightstand, I lean back against my pillows and prop my head up on my arm. My chest hurts just thinking how quickly the tables turned on her when she didn't do anything to deserve it.

I've been a complete ass to her the past few days and all she's trying to do is continue working a job she loves.

Closing my eyes, I remind myself that when Jesse needed a job, we found a place for him. We hired Alex to revamp all our websites. Taking those tasks off our plates has freed us up to expand our business. Hiring Reese will also enable us to do that as well.

Her softness will offset my gruffness nicely; I think, with a little trust, we can be a good team. The question is, am I ready to trust someone with something so important to me? My business is everything. It's what got me through the heartbreak of Cece's deception.

It doesn't matter that this situation is different. From the moment I shook Reese's hand, I could feel a connection between us and that feeling scares me, it's something I didn't even feel with Cece. And when she was talking, the fierce protectiveness that surged through me, it was overwhelming and new.

Scrubbing my hands over my face, I sigh. "It was nothing, just a natural instinct."

My voice is loud in my room, but I need to tell myself I would feel that way about anyone in the same situation.

Even if it is a lie.

Picking up my cell, I call Jesse. When his voice greets me through the speaker, I stand up and grab my wallet and keys off my dresser. "Want to go to Linger with me?"

Instead of dwelling on this woman and the prickly uncomfortable feeling that comes along with thoughts of her, I need a beer and someone up for a good time. Jesse is the lesser of evils when I think of my social circle. Besides, he's so hung up on Ashton, maybe he needs to get that off his chest too.

An hour later, Jesse and I each have a beer in hand as we gaze around Linger. It's packed, the dance floor pulsing with people moving to the mix the DJ is playing. I notice a blonde woman dancing with her friends, but her eyes keep wandering to me.

Smiling, I wink at her before turning my attention to Jesse. "How are things going on the home front?"

"Do you mean with my father who still refuses to acknowledge me? Or my unrequited crush on my roommate?"

"I'm talking about the clearly requited crush on your roommate." Smirking as he gapes at me, I take a swig of beer before continuing, "He's just waiting for you to be ready, but if you're too shy to let him know how you're feeling, he's going to move on."

He doesn't say anything but downs the rest of his beer. This is how Jesse works, he can be completely oblivious, but once he makes a decision he goes for it without looking back.

Leaning against the bar, I glance back toward the blonde, smiling when her gaze keeps finding mine.

Jesse orders another beer, but I wave him off. I want to be able to drive home later, I never spend the night with any of the women I hook up with, it leads to unrealistic expectations.

It doesn't take long for the blonde to start making her way over to me. Her brilliant red lips part to show a perfect set of teeth. It's even better that her smile is genuine and reaches her eyes.

"I'm Sarah." She holds out her hand, which I take, my smile becoming a bit more forced when I don't feel any sort of excitement.

"Ryan. Can I buy you a drink?"

She nods, her soft voice ordering a beer. I second that, needing something to do with my hands. I've never felt awkward in this situation, but right now something feels off and the visual of Reese popping into my head unsettles me.

I try to listen to what Sarah is saying, but it doesn't take long for me to realize this won't go anywhere. Jesse must see it because he appears, putting me out of my misery.

"Hey, man, I just got a text from Dane. Samson broke out and they need a hand wrangling him."

A mixture of relief and frustration at myself floods through me as I apologize to Sarah and get out of there.

Jesse follows me out, but we head our separate ways without a word.

Thirty minutes later, I'm in bed, thinking about Reese.

As I drift off, the image of her smile sends me into dreamland.

CHAPTER SIX

My alarm beeps, rousing me from another rough night's sleep. Ugh, why did I set it for six in the morning? Turning it off, I roll over and close my eyes again, except sleep eludes me.

Sasha. That's why.

I've been too tired the last couple of days to spend any time with her.

Groaning, I roll out of bed and get ready for the day. The delicious scent of coffee greets me as I stumble out of my room, still a little bleary-eyed. At least I had the foresight to set the machine.

I grab an apple, pour coffee in a travel mug, and I'm out the door before I can talk myself into sleeping for a couple more hours. Ryan said we didn't need to start until nine today since we only have two clients and they're not far from each other. This time, I get to go by myself.

My stomach twists. I'm a little nervous, I want to impress

the clients, so they have good things to say about me when Ryan calls and asks how I did, because I suspect he will.

Devouring my apple, I offer the core to Sasha who chomps it up with a happy whoosh of horse breath in my face. It's a little stinky, which reminds me I need to have her teeth done.

Add that to the list of things I can't afford.

Shaking it off, I drink my coffee as I head into the shop to grab my tack. Ryan left a key under the mat so I could let myself in until he makes it to town to have one cut for me.

Twenty minutes later, I'm sitting in the saddle and trotting lazy circles in a round pen behind the barn. Tension rolls off my shoulders as the cool morning air fills my lungs. Rolling my hips, I loosen up and then nudge her into a lope.

This feeling, the one of freedom and hope racing through my veins as I ride, this is why I'm here. It's why I keep fighting and don't give up. Being up here, seeing the world from a different perspective as I feel Sasha move so gracefully with me, it reminds me that my time isn't over. I can recoup from the last seven years. I can pay off my debt, rebuild my career... *find love again.* It doesn't matter how difficult it is or how scary, I'm a fighter and I won't let anything beat me down.

"Hello! You must be Reese." A soft, feminine voice startles me. Sasha prances to the side when I accidentally dig into her flank. "Oh, I'm so sorry, I thought you saw me."

I focus on the person talking to me. A pretty woman with dark brown hair smiles and waves. She looks so friendly and warm, I can't help but smile in return. "Good morning! I didn't really expect to see anyone so early."

She smirks, glancing at the cell she holds in her hand. "Early? It's eight-thirty."

Gaping, I trot over and she shows me the time. "Oh shit."

I swing off Sasha's back, landing with a thud in the dirt.

"I can't believe I lost track of time." My voice cracks. I'm so flustered, I try and fail twice at the snap on the gate before she opens it for me.

"Girl, you're fine. If anyone is going to understand how easy it is to lose yourself when you're riding, it's any of us." She grins at me. "I'm Lia, by the way. I popped by to introduce myself, give you the passcode for the garage so you can get into the laundry room to wash your clothes, and schedule a time to work on this gorgeous mare of yours."

She talks a mile a minute, it takes me a moment to process. "Lia. Right, I forgot you were coming by. It's nice to meet you. Thank you so much for taking on Sasha, she's been a little sore lately and anything to help."

We walk together back to the pen next to my apartment, Lia watching how Sasha moves. She's observant, her face serious. A complete contrast to the bubbly woman who greeted me.

By the time we get to the pen, she's rattling off all the things she wants to do.

"I think if we work on her once a week, say Fridays, she will be in tip-top shape. She's actually not so bad, just needs a little adjusting." Lia opens the gate for me, watching as I work. "The garage code is two-six-five-eight. The door to the laundry room is always unlocked, so feel free to pop in. I was thinking Thursdays, if that works for you?"

"That all sounds great." I will agree to anything, I'm just so grateful to be here and she's being so kind to me, just like Dane. Now, I just need to win over Ryan and I'll be set.

"Perfect. When you're settled, we have breakfast as a group every weekday, but since you live on the property you're also invited for weekends. It's at the main house at seven, unless otherwise coordinated. Also, we have a girls' night twice a month, and we would love it if you would join us. We alternate whose house we have it at, I believe the next one is next Friday at Emma's house. I have to check, baby brain and all that fun stuff." She bubbles, her hand resting on her stomach.

There is the smallest bump under her hand. I smile, but my heart is breaking a little. I always wanted to have a family, but Justin wasn't ready in the early years of our marriage which turned out to be a blessing, but now I feel like my time is running out.

"Wow, congrats!" It's an exciting time for her, and if I can show Ryan I'm an asset to the ranch and to his business, maybe I will get to meet her baby.

"Thanks! Anyway, I should let you get to work before Ryan comes searching. I'll see you Friday for our appointment, unless of course you join us for breakfast tomorrow." She turns and walks with me in the direction of the shop, despite her goodbye, talking the entire way about different things happening at the ranch over the next month.

By the time I'm standing inside the shop and she's disappeared, I'm still reeling from the velocity that words flowed from her tiny body.

Ryan looks up from where he's rooting around in his desk. "You look like you got hit by a whirlwind. I'm guessing you met Lia." He chuckles.

Nodding, I eye him warily. What's going on today? Why is he smiling at me?

"I did. She's nice—energetic." I return his smile, still curious what brought on this change of attitude.

He gestures next to him at the chair. "Why don't we get yesterday's invoice done and then you can head out. I suppose I can prep the invoices for today's clients that way we can send them right away."

He sighs, rolling his eyes but he's smiling.

I don't understand what's going on, but I don't want to ask and ruin it.

"Did you arrange laundry and an appointment for Sasha with Lia?" He glances at me as the program loads.

"We did."

"And did she invite you to breakfast?" He returns his attention to the computer, scrolling through and updating the client's file before duplicating the invoice. It hasn't changed since the last time, so I suggested yesterday that we duplicate instead of redoing the paperwork.

"She did." I shrug, but the offer meant a lot to me. Aside from my family, no one from my previous social circle speaks to me. It was eye opening at how superficial my friendships were.

"So, are you going to come to breakfast?" He leans back after sending the invoice. His tone is friendly, casual. Completely different from our previous exchanges.

"Ummm, yeah, one day." I get up from my chair and start packing up my things. The idea of fully immersing myself in their lives is appealing, but I'm a little gun shy from years of being a social pariah.

"You should come tomorrow. Everyone will be there, it's a good chance to meet the rest of the people who work on the ranch. Think of it as a welcome to the team breakfast." He gets up, wincing when he smacks his broken arm against the edge of the desk, but he holds my gaze until I nod.

"Okay, I will be there tomorrow." Smiling, I try to tamp down the nerves. It doesn't matter how old I get, the eagerness to make a good impression on people hasn't subsided.

I finish packing up and set my route with a grin on my face. Today is shaping up to be fantastic. I guess it's finally time for something to go right.

~

Cringing as I park my car and see who's waiting for me, I regret my optimism this morning. Everything has been going so well too. The previous client was this sweet older lady who made me lunch and then sent me on my way with a tin full of chocolate chip cookies.

And then I see *her*. Now, I can't honestly remember her name, and the file has their last name listed, a name I was never given, but I recognize her. She hooked up with Justin about a year into our divorce proceedings. She slept with him while she was married. To the man standing next to her.

As I hop out of my car, I paste on a smile and pretend I don't know who she is.

"Hi, Mister and Missus Johnstone! It's so lovely to meet you!" My voice is chipper as I step forward to greet them.

We exchange pleasantries, well, he's pleasant, she's glaring daggers at me whenever he's not looking. A sick feeling settles into my stomach, I know this isn't going to end well for me.

I pray that Mr. Johnstone will stick around, so at least I have someone there to witness me at work.

"Well, I have to go back to the field." He leaves, along with my sense of hope.

As soon as he's out of hearing range, all pretenses fall away.

"Well, well, well. I see you're back at work. I'm shocked the Hyatt's hired you, what with the stain on your name." Her lips curl back into a sneer.

"Look, I'm just here to do my job. I don't have any intention of doing or saying anything that isn't related to your horses' hoof health." I try to speak in a low, soft tone. I can see the fear in her eyes, and fear makes people do rash and cruel things.

She scoffs, muttering to herself.

I grab my tools and thank my lucky stars they only have two horses. Putting my entire focus on my work, I try to ignore the rude and condescending remarks coming my way. Any

time she directly addresses me, I respond in a polite, professional manner while trying to work as fast as I possibly can.

"You know, you never deserved Justin. The way you treated
him, taking everything from him. And then you play the victim
when people finally start being honest about your shitty work.
People only tolerated you because of him." Her voice is cold,
biting. "I never did see what he saw in you."

By the time I'm done, I'm shaking. I give her the biggest
smile I can muster. "All done. Ryan will send you the invoice as
well as schedule the next appointment."

"Oh, there won't be a next appointment. Ryan will be
hearing from me. Your quality of work is pathetic, and I won't
work with anyone that has you on their payroll." She pulls out
her phone, giving me a pointed look as she starts to dial. She
lifts it to her ear, sauntering away as it begins to ring.

Loading up my tools, I clench my teeth and breathe deeply
through my nose. My hands are trembling as I drive away,
fighting the tears that threaten. I refuse to cry because of her.

CHAPTER SEVEN

Ryan

Hanging up the phone, I stare blankly, trying to process everything I just heard. I have to work my jaw to unclench it, but nothing is going to calm me down right now.

Sandy Johnstone has been a client of mine for about two and a half years now. She and her husband religiously book their horses for trimming and re-shoeing every six weeks. Reese goes there one time and costs me their business.

Sandy's criticisms echo in my thoughts.

She was completely unprofessional. Rude to me. Rough with my horses. Their hooves look worse than they did prior to the trim.

Those weren't the worst ones though. The worst one, the one that hit right on the nerve was *"It makes me question what kind of business would hire someone like that. What kind of low standards you're now setting for your staff and their quality of work."*

Those words hit me right where it hurts, because that was

my fear. What was I thinking letting her go on her own after only a few days? I was sucked in by the glowing reviews. Now I've been taken for a fool, and I hate looking like a fool. Even worse, I hate that I now have this stain on my name.

Sandy is not a quiet woman, and I know she will be spouting off to whomever will listen about how she's no longer using my services because she's not happy with my staff.

After pacing around my shop as I fume, I decide to be proactive and call the other client she saw today, to get their feedback so when I talk to her I can be fully informed about how the day went. As I pick up the phone to call, I hear tires crunching over the gravel driveway and when I look out the open door of my shop, I spot my business truck.

Reese parks the truck in its spot. I forgot I told her to take the company truck and not her own. I groan. She's been driving around with my name plastered on the side of the vehicle all day.

Sitting in my chair, I take a deep breath and attempt to calm down while she grabs her things. When she walks in the door, shutting it behind her, I can see she's not smiling. It's almost as though she knows, but how could she?

"I received a disturbing phone call from Sandy Johnstone forty-five minutes ago." My voice is cold and if Dane were here he'd be giving me the "you need to calm down and be professional look," so I take a deep breath and try for a more neutral tone, but before I can continue Reese rushes in.

"I know. And I would like the chance to explain." She's looking at me pleadingly, strain written across her face.

"What's there to explain? I told you that you represent me and my family's name and business. I trusted you to act professionally and meet high standards of work that I expect from myself and anyone working for me. The past few days I thought I saw that quality of work from you. And then Sandy called. She was incredibly upset with how you spoke to her, how you handled her horses, and the poor state of her horses' hooves. She told me that she will no longer require my company's services, that she will find a new farrier. For over two years, I haven't had any problems or complaints, and after one appointment with you, she's gone. That's a loss of three hundred dollars every six weeks." My tone is biting, the neutrality gone as I get angrier with each word I speak.

"Ryan, please just let me tell you my side of it." Her voice is steady, calm. When I glance down though, her hands are shaking.

"There is no other side. The customer is always right. I told Dane it was a mistake to hire someone. I told him we could recommend a friend of mine to take on our clients until my arm is healed, but he wanted to expand, and now I've lost business." I shove my chair back and stand up, shaking my head. There is no justification for this.

Reese purses her lips, her eyes narrowing. "There is another side and you need to listen to it." She raises her voice to just below a shout, moving to stand between me and the door.

Widening my stance, I gape at her. I haven't been the most pleasant guy and she's just taken it, but I can tell by the determined look on her face she's not going to let this go.

"Fine, if you think it makes a difference, let me hear it."

"Sandy Johnstone was fucking my ex-husband while we were in the process of getting divorced. She was married to her husband at the time, but Justin was her side piece until he tossed her aside. She's a known buckle bunny, waiting to hook her claws in someone before she leaves her husband, because he's just a simple farmer."

Reese's tone is void of emotion, but her eyes paint a story of loneliness and pain. I recognize the look from when Lia and

Graham broke up. Hell, I recognize it in the face I look at in the mirror every damn day. She continues in the same flat voice, "I could see the fear that I would out her from the moment we locked eyes. The only thing I said to her is that I was there to do my job and that's it. From the moment I 'met' her and her husband, I treated them with nothing but respect, despite the verbal abuse I endured from her the entire time I worked with their horses. I guarantee if you go and look at those horses' feet, you will be more than satisfied with my performance. Now, if you do go there and you're not happy with my work, then take disciplinary action. Until then, I need to go lay down because I don't deserve to be treated this way and I refuse to tolerate it."

I'm silent as she puts her tools away with her usual care, deep in thought as I watch her leave the shop.

Picking up my phone, I call Mark's cell.

"Hey, Ryan. How's the arm feeling?" Mark's voice is pleasant, the sound of a tractor rumbling in the background.

"It's okay, just annoying. I wanted to call and get your impression of Reese, and to see if I could swing by and check out your horses' hooves, make sure they look okay." I work hard to keep the irritation out of my voice, but I'm not sure I'm successful.

The rumbling turns off, Mark's voice laced with concern replies, "Of course. Sandy just left, but I'm taking a break for the next hour if you want to swing by. Reese seemed like a nice enough person, I didn't stick around for the trim, I let Sandy stand with the horses so I could work."

We end the call with a promise from me that I will be there before he ends his break.

Forty-five minutes later, I'm parking my truck next to the horse corral the two horses are currently eating in. Mark appears from inside the barn, smiling happily. He's a good-natured fellow, the complete opposite of Sandy. She's always come across as a little high maintenance, but I never had any issues with her.

Mark stands by curiously as I let myself into the pen. The horses walk over to greet me, nuzzling my pockets for treats. I bend down and awkwardly pick up a hoof, inspecting it.

It's perfect.

"She's as good as you," Mark comments as he peers over my shoulder. "What's this about, Ryan? It seems like a waste of your time to be driving out here to inspect Reese's work."

Before I can answer, another car pulls up. Sandy gets out, the smirk on her face falling when she sees me drop the hoof I'm holding. Her skin paling under her summer tan.

I answer Mark loud enough so Sandy can hear. "I couldn't be here during your trim appointment earlier today. Since Reese is new, I'm just following up with my clients to ensure she's the right fit for a permanent position on my team."

We leave the pen, stopping outside my truck. "I have to say, based on what I've seen here and at other client's, she's an excellent addition to our team. I don't think I need to follow up anymore." I turn my gaze onto Sandy, her silent behavior speaking volumes.

"She was fine, quiet but polite. Right, sweetheart?" Mark wraps his arm around Sandy as she joins us.

She avoids my gaze as she murmurs her agreement.

"Good. Well, I better get back to the shop. Thanks for letting me come by, Mark. I will let Reese know you're happy with her work. I trust our regular six-week schedule is still working for you?"

"Absolutely." Mark shakes my hand and steps back as I open my truck door, Sandy still not meeting my gaze.

Hopping in my truck, I make the forty-five-minute drive home, guilt settling into my gut. I'm better than this, I'm better than how I've been treating Reese and the quickness with which I doubt her and her professionalism. I don't need to know her well to know she works hard. Her recommendation from Roy and the work I witnessed the past couple of days is enough. Especially yesterday.

I'm ashamed of myself and my behavior.

Instead of heading home, I turn down the driveway to the shop and park next to her truck. Preparing myself to eat humble pie, I knock on her door and wait.

There's no movement inside and no answer when I knock a couple more times.

Glancing over, I notice Sasha isn't in her pen. Hiking through the barn to the indoor arena, I spend the next thirty minutes trying to find her, but she's disappeared. Likely exploring one of the many trails we have throughout the ranch.

Heading back to my truck, I promise myself I'll make things right tomorrow.

Instead of going into the house when I get home, I walk over to Emma and Dane's. Just in case Reese approaches him, I want him to know I'm fixing the situation.

This ought to be fun.

CHAPTER EIGHT

Reese

My alarm goes off, reminding me I agreed to go to the main house for breakfast this morning. Turning it off, I roll over and close my eyes. Like hell I want to sit through breakfast with Ryan glaring at me in that unwavering, uncaring way. Working through it is bad enough. Pile on the false sense of happiness I experienced yesterday morning only to have it ripped away the same day and I just want to spend some time not feeling like shit.

When will my relationship with Justin quit haunting me? When will I finally get to find my happy after years of feeling lost and defeated? I feel like no matter what I do, I just can't get my head above water.

I saw Ryan leave shortly after I left the shop yesterday, hopefully to go and check out my work. If not, I don't know if I can continue to work in an environment where my every step is going to be doubted and criticized. I don't want to leave, I don't want to give up, but I deserve better. At least, I keep reminding myself I do, because I need to hear it from someone and who better than myself.

It's amazing what years of abuse does to your self-esteem. When I took this job, I promised myself I would fake confidence until it ceased to be fake, but Ryan's attitude makes it nearly impossible.

This is supposed to be my fresh start, working for a family-centric business that treats its employees with care and support. It feels like I'm standing on the ground as it crumbles beneath me. Completely out of control.

I lay in bed, trying to quiet my mind. We don't have any clients today since Ryan had to book a couple on Saturday, which gives me more time to prepare myself for seeing him again.

When I can't fall back asleep, I roll out of bed and make a pot of coffee. Grabbing my eReader, I open the new book I bought. I'm about to immerse myself in a fictional world with badass women warriors defeating a tribe of an opposing clan when there is a soft knock on my door.

My heart beats a little faster, but instead of ignoring it, I set my tablet aside and cross the short distance to the door. Slowly opening it, I look up into Ryan's rich brown eyes.

He must've went to the Johnstone's based off the remorseful look on his face. His voice is soft when he asks, "May I please come in?"

My hand squeezes the door as I search his expression for any hint that this is going to be another disappointing interaction. What I see is a little vulnerability, genuine vulnerability, so I step back, opening the door further to let him in.

He glances down, his eyes widening, before he averts his eyes. "I'm so sorry, I didn't think about the early hour. Were you sleeping?"

I look down, blushing when I remember I'm wearing tiny sleep shorts that are basically underwear and a tight, white tank top. "Oh God!" Running into my room, I throw on a pair of sweats and a hoodie.

Running my hands over my face, I attempt to calm my pulse and pray that my color is back to normal.

Rejoining Ryan in the living room, I walk back to the chair I was sitting in without a word. Tucking my knees into my chest, I silently watch as he sits in the chair next to me.

"Reese, I owe you so many apologies for my behavior and I'm not going to attempt to give a blanket apology. Before I get into everything, I just need to say that I was completely in the wrong yesterday." He runs a hand through his hair, grimacing. "I went to the Johnstone's after you left the shop. The hooves were perfect and as soon as Sandy saw me, I could see it in her expression that everything she said when she called was out of some sort of petty vendetta, just like you told me."

Nodding, I feel my body relax. At least my integrity is no longer in question.

"I don't think I need to outline my poor behavior over the past few days, unless you would like me to?" He waits until I shake my head. "I promise that, from now on, I will be the boss I should've been from the very start. And I would like to make it up to you."

"Ryan, that's not really necessary." My voice is soft. I drop one foot to the floor and lean forward. "I just want us to have a good working relationship, if we can do that, then everything else is forgotten."

"I won't forget it, especially—" He pauses, but I already know what he's thinking. Especially given my history. "Nevertheless, I thought I could show you around the property on horseback. I know today is the day you arranged to come by the house to do laundry. Why don't we meet at one, that way you have some time beforehand?" He smiles at me and I see the Ryan I was expecting from the moment I accepted this job.

"What about your arm?"

Ryan gives me a wry smile. "Don't worry about it, I can manage one-handed."

He stands up before I can argue, his remorse written all over his face. Maybe spending some non-work time with him will enable us to find a new beginning. We obviously have a lot in common and I would like to be on friendly terms with him instead of this up and down turmoil. I believe him when he promises he will change his tune, but I also believed this morning was a turning point when he greeted me with a completely different attitude.

Only time will tell. He gets one last chance.

"Okay. One works," I promise softly.

He looks at me without saying anything for a moment before turning and letting himself out with a gruff goodbye.

In the time between when Ryan left and the time I'm supposed to meet him, I get two loads of laundry washed, dried, and put away and still have time to pace my apartment.

Now, I'm sitting outside the main house on Sasha, impressed by the sheer magnitude of the ranch and the scope of their services. Looking around, I see Lia riding a horse through the glass windows of an enormous outdoor arena, and a guy leaning against the fence in obvious displeasure.

As I watch, I hear the barn doors slide open and out comes Ryan leading a beautiful palomino. He smiles at me, the warmth of it sending shivers down my spine. I was too nervous the day we met to feel the full force of his charm, but I can't seem to look away at how striking he is when he's not scowling at me.

"Sasha really is a beautiful horse." He walks up along side of me to give her a gentle pat, before turning and mounting his horse one-handed, staying steady in the stirrups when she prances to the side. "This is Joy. She's one of the horses that Dane is training. She hasn't been on the trails before and this is only her tenth ride. Dane doesn't know I'm taking her out because he wouldn't approve." His eyes twinkle mischievously. I feel a little bad for his family, I can't imagine it's easy to wrangle him into taking proper care of himself.

"I haven't been on a green horse in so long." The words come out longingly as I watch him work her through the excitement of being out in the open, his right arm nestled into his chest. Before my divorce, I had a friend that trained horses and I used to help out. Of course, she was another person who dropped me when Justin started spreading vicious lies about me.

"If you like, you can ride her back at the end of our tour." Ryan finally has her standing still, even with her tail swishing in agitation he looks completely at ease. "Ready?"

Nodding, I follow as he nudges Joy forward.

He leads us down a trail, Joy prancing this way and that as she explores new ground. She's doing quite well, just excited and quick.

I can't help but admire Ryan's patience, his posture relaxed but controlled, and the sheer amount of skill as he works through her quirks with one arm out of commission. He's kind to her even as he corrects her. It's a testament to the real Ryan I've only caught a glimpse of.

We wind through the trails, Joy settling into a nice pace. She's quite the impressive horse and if I were in the market for a second one, I would be making an offer.

"So, how did you come across Sasha? She's the most magnificent Appaloosa I've ever seen." Ryan slows Joy so we're walking side by side.

"It was actually a happy accident. You see, she was solid black when she was born, and the breeder wasn't happy with her conformation. Anyway, I was at a horse conference and they had her picture tucked away beneath others for sale. There was something I saw in her eyes and I asked about her. They basically said she was a 'throw away' horse and I could take her home that day for just five-hundred dollars. Thankfully, she was registered prior to this decision, which was incredibly lucky for me." Pausing, I look over at him and grin. "Within six months, she shed away some of the black hair to reveal the white. She steadied and revealed that her conformation isn't flawed, and it became evident I got a steal of a deal. The next year, I went back and showed them her photo. You should've seen the look on their faces. I don't think they've made such a rash decision again."

Ryan laughs. "That's quite the story."

"Yeah, we've had this special bond from the moment I loaded her in my trailer and took her home. She got me through my divorce. Justin and I separated shortly after I got her which almost caused me to lose her. When I left Justin after finally having enough and realizing I needed to quit making excuses for him, I discovered that he racked up a ton of debt in my name. I was able to arrange a payment plan, but they were stripping me of my assets." My blood boils when I think of all Justin cost me. "I hid her, my truck, and my trailer with Roy, he bought me out before the bank could take them. He's the only reason I didn't have to sell them to put toward the debt."

"I'm glad Roy helped you out. By the sounds of it you got

screwed in your divorce." Ryan's voice is cutting, Joy prancing a little as he tenses in the saddle.

Chuckling, I try not to be bitter, but it's hard not to. "Yeah, and definitely not in the enjoyable way."

The words fly out of my mouth, my face flushing as I process what I've just said to my boss. Thankfully, Ryan throws his head back and laughs.

"Well, silver lining is it's done now, right? Nowhere to go but up." He glances over at me with a friendly grin, my own lips twitch in response despite the topic.

"Yeah." I lean down and pat Sasha. "Nowhere to go but up."

The rest of the ride I slowly get to know Ryan. I learn he's fiercely protective of his family. That Dane and Emma are getting married. Lia and Alex are having a baby. Which leaves Ryan, as the eldest, in the crosshairs of his mother's attention. It's apparent the entire family is close, and they run the ranch like a well-oiled machine, expanding but only when it makes good business sense.

Hearing him talk about the ranch, the passion in his voice and the pride that emanates from him as he goes over the different facets, makes me feel good about following my instincts to come here. Those instincts haven't always been kind to me, but maybe this time I got it right.

As we pass another large corral, this one empty, Ryan stops Joy and dismounts.

"So, what do you think, want to ride her the rest of the way back? That is, if you feel comfortable with leaving Sasha with me." He watches as I fight a smile.

My stomach flutters in excitement as I hop down and we exchange reins. "Heck yes, I want to ride her!"

We both get back in the saddle, Ryan nudging Sasha to lead the way. Joy is prancy in the excitable way many green horses are, but she responds to the lightest pressure and seems eager to please.

"If you ever want to check out the ranch in its entirety, we'd need to plan for a weekend. The ranch is currently three hundred and twenty acres." Ryan's casualness when mentioning how many acres the family owns stuns me.

"Three twenty? Currently? Are you thinking of expanding?"

He smirks at the shock in my voice. "One of our neighbors is recently widowed. He's talked about moving closer to his kids, I told him before he decides to put his farm on the market to call me first. He has six hundred and forty acres, so if it works out we would expand to nine sixty."

I'm speechless. Words fail me as I correct Joy when she tries to pick up speed without my cue. I can't even imagine. The idea of that much land is... "Wow." I finally manage to form a word.

"We're always looking at ways to expand the business, and his farm is set up for hay, which means we could rent it out to a farmer, quit growing our own but still have hay grown on the property. I've had some ideas rolling around in my head, but I haven't really finalized any of them yet, not until we know for sure what's happening."

By listening to Ryan, I'm not paying close enough attention to Joy or our surroundings, so when a huge moose comes barreling through the trees and stops in the path before us, I'm not prepared for her to rear up. Thankfully, I keep my seat as it continues on its destructive path, paying us no mind.

Joy prances, her head high, snorting as she spins and takes off in the opposite direction. Sinking into the saddle, I coo at her as I focus on slowly bringing her back to me. Without increasing the pressure too much, I gently pull on the reins to remind her I'm with her and get her to slow to a trot and then a walk.

Finally, we stop. Her flank heaves from the exertion, but her head lowers as she lets out a huge breath. Turning her, I softly nudge her into a walk as we head back in the direction we left Ryan.

Rounding a bend, I see Ryan and Sasha cantering toward us, Ryan's expression transforms into one of relief when he sees the two of us unharmed.

"Are you okay?" His voice is deeper than normal, his eyes checking me over to make sure I'm not harmed, leaving a blazing path of heat in their wake.

"We're fine. She was in flight mode, it took a minute to get her to remember me, but when she did she came down nicely." Leaning down, I pat Joy on the neck, smiling as she lets out another deep breath.

"I'm impressed. I better watch out, Dane might steal you for the training program." He turns Sasha, waiting until we're plodding along next to each other.

"Anywhere you need me, just let me know." I sound a little breathless, the excitement still rushing through my veins. "I'm going to need things to fill my time."

"Well, the space around the apartment is yours if you like gardening or anything like that. We also have a pretty decent woodworking shop. And I wasn't kidding, once you're settled into a routine with clients and if you're interested, I'm sure Dane would love an extra hand with the colts he's working."

CHAPTER NINE

Ryan

After dropping Reese off at home, I ride Joy back to the training barn. Dismounting, I tie her, putting her tack away before giving her a good grooming.

Reese and I spent close to two hours on the trail. Seeing her smile at me, watching the tension she carries on her shoulders slowly dissipate felt surprisingly good. The smile she gave me before I left her with Sasha highlighted just how beautiful she is, inside and out. The way she forgave me, I know I didn't deserve it, but her heart is too kind to hold a grudge.

I also see how she ended up tolerating that dipshit of an ex's bullshit for so long. The fact that I can find parallels in his behavior to mine over the past couple of days is disturbing and something I need to reflect on. I don't want to be an angry and hateful guy.

"Your arm is never going to heal if you keep using it like that," Dane says as he comes out of the supplement room, a half-eaten apple in hand. He continues when I ignore him. "How'd she do?"

Patting Joy on the neck, I grin over at him. "Good. She's got some speed."

Dane takes a bite out of his apple, raising his brows as he waits for more information. Filling him in on what happened with the moose and Joy taking off with Reese on her back, I can see the wheels turning in his head as I mention how well Reese handled it.

"I told her you might want some help once she's settled and we know it's going to work out. You know, when she's not with clients." Seeing the interest in his eyes, my stomach twists a little in a weird sensation. It's not enjoyable.

Dane follows me out of the barn to the paddock Joy shares with another mare. "Yeah, I mean obviously your clients are priority, but it sounds like she's a skilled rider and definitely having some help with these guys would be great. Let's give her time to adjust and we can go from there." He pauses, watching me for a minute. Observing me. His eyes flash in amusement at whatever he sees. It's annoying. "I'm glad you were able to straighten things out with her. It's nice to see you putting in an effort."

"I guess I realized it's what we do, we did the same thing for Jesse and that's worked out well. Everyone here has a role, and I think Reese could do well. Besides, she needs it, maybe more than we even know." Shrugging, I follow Dane back into the barn and help him clean up.

"Agreed." Dane looks thoughtful as he grabs a manure fork to start cleaning stalls. "Should we invite her to Lia's show this weekend?"

I hand him the shovel to scoop some clean woodchips once he's done and ponder his question. "No. She's just got here, she doesn't really know any of us, we should let her get settled in."

He nods in agreement. "We should at least make sure she comes for breakfast tomorrow, meet everyone before we all head off."

Knocking on Reese's door for the second time today, I grin when I think about this morning. She's toned yet feminine, the flush on her face filling my head with images of her being laid out beneath me. It's totally inappropriate, but I can't seem to turn off that part of my brain. Not when I know she's available, and I'm still not certain she'd be an unwilling partner.

The door swings open, this time she's not half-naked, but I'm positive she was sleeping.

"Crap, I really have terrible timing, don't I?" Glancing at the time on my cell, I see it's not even ten o'clock yet. I got distracted at dinner by Lia and Alex arguing over Lia's show that I almost forgot my promise to make sure Reese comes for breakfast tomorrow.

"It's okay, I just haven't been sleeping well so I was attempting to catch up." She yawns, her voice scratchy. Her hair is sticking up wildly around her head, I tuck my hands in my pockets to resist smoothing it. "What's wrong?"

"Nothing's wrong. I just wanted to make sure you remembered the standing invitation for breakfast at the main house. You only get so much time before Lia will make it mandatory, she says it's a great way to start our day and reinforce comradery. Plus, she wants Jesse and Nella and you to remember you're a part of the family too." Smiling fondly, I recall when she threatened to hog-tie Emma.

"Oh, yeah. I'll make sure to show up." She sways on her feet, obviously exhausted, her hand barely holding her up from where it grasps the frame.

"Is there anything we can do to make the apartment more comfortable?" Concern fills me, but she waves it off.

"No. I realized when I moved in here that I've always lived with someone else. It's an adjustment being in a home by myself. I love it but combining that with a new space and learning the sounds, it's been a rough few nights. It's all good." She smiles at me. "If that's all?"

"Oh, right. Just come on in the house tomorrow, the kitchen is easy to find. And. Yeah. Goodnight. I hope you sleep well."

She gives me another tired smile before shutting the door. I wait until I hear the lock turn before heading home.

The kitchen smells like bacon and coffee, making my stomach growl as I grab a mug and pour myself a cup of coffee. Everyone is here this morning, except Reese.

Taking my seat next to Jesse, I meet Lia's eyes and shrug, trying to pretend I'm not disappointed.

Before I can grab a waffle, the kitchen door opens and Reese's head pokes in. Her hair is tied up in a messy bun, strands flying all over the place as she gives us all a sheepish grin.

"Sorry I'm late. I slept through my alarm." She spies the empty chair next to me and crosses the room to sit down.

"No worries!" Lia's chipper response fills the room. "I don't think you've met everyone. So, we have, Jesse, Nella, Emma, and Alex. You of course know Dane, me, and Ryan."

Introductions done, we all fill our plates, chatter filling the room as we discuss Lia's show this weekend. Reese listens with amusement as Alex frets over Lia who is clearly getting exasperated by him.

Leaning over I whisper, "She looks ready to dump syrup on his head."

Reese chuckles, the soft sound is low and throaty. The sexy type of chuckle that hits you straight in the gut. "I think it's sweet. He loves her and their baby so much, it's apparent in the adoration in his eyes. My parents have that look when they talk to each other. My sister and brother-in-law too. If I think about it, I don't believe Justin ever did. To have someone who looks at you with complete and utter love like that, it's something worth having."

Nella accidentally bumps Reese, drawing her attention, the poor girl stumbles over an apology. As they strike up a conversation, I sit there reeling.

How can she have gone through what she did, and still think about love without wanting to throw up? I've seen so many sides to her in such a short time, I can tell she's guarded, but there's an openness, a willingness to put herself out there and try again that is admirable.

"Ryan, are you still planning to join us tomorrow?" Lia's voice breaks into my thoughts.

Glancing up, I laugh when I see her hand covering Alex's mouth. "Yeah. But first, I want to get August booked, so I need to follow up with all the clients who were kind of on hold." Turning to Reese, I say, "You might have a really busy few weeks, some of them are a little behind."

She smiles, her eyes lighting up. "Sounds perfect. Being busy doing something you love is no hardship."

Dane catches my eye with an "I told you so" look. I roll my eyes in reply.

"So, Reese, how're you settling in?" Emma rests her hand on Dane's arm, smiling. It still shocks me how much she's changed in the last year, from the dejected woman who showed up here to the glowing one engaged to my brother.

"I'm unpacked and settled. It was a pretty easy move."

She lays her cutlery down on her plate, her cheeks flushing a little under the scrutiny of everyone. What she's leaving out is that she doesn't have a lot to begin with. It's admirable that instead of focusing on what's gone wrong in her life, she focuses on moving forward. Sometimes it's so easy to continuously fall into the negativity trap and try and garnish pity at every turn.

"Did Lia tell you about our girls' night? We have them every month and we'd love for you to join us," Emma presses.

"Yeah, that sounds fun." Reese's voice lacks the usual enthusiasm Emma and Lia have when they talk about their girls' nights and it doesn't go unnoticed. They exchange glances, their smiles falling a little.

An awkward silence descends on the table, causing Reese to flush even more.

Reese tries again by saying, "It does sound fun. I'm sorry, it's been a long time, that's all."

The girls fill in the blanks and their expressions morph into ones of excitement again. "It's definitely time to rectify that!"

They obviously were able to read between the lines, because I know when those two are scheming and the looks they're sharing are full of unspoken plans. At least their schemes almost always work out and are a ton of fun.

After breakfast, I clear out of the kitchen along with Dane and Jesse. I haven't gone with them to fix fences and do routine checks since I broke my arm. I hate feeling out of the loop. Even worse is feeling like I'm not contributing.

Helping as much as I can, I watch them ride away before hopping in my truck and heading to the shop. Just before the driveway opens into the parking space, I notice a little shaking bundle of white on the side of the road. Stopping, I hop out and approach with caution until I see it's a scared Jack Russell tied to a tree. My blood boils.

Its body vibrates as I approach, reminding me to take a few calming breaths before I crouch low and untie the poor thing. Using my good hand to let it sniff me before scooping under its belly, I carry it to my truck. It's not the first time someone has abandoned animals on our property.

In my truck I check her over and to my relief other than being a little dirty, a little skinny, and a lot scared, she's okay.

Pulling into my usual spot, I scoop her up and carry her into my open shop door.

Reese turns, her eyes widening when she sees the dog. "I didn't know you had a dog."

"I don't. This little girl was tied to a tree on the driveway. It's a good thing I drove my truck instead of one of the quads, otherwise I would've missed her, and she would've been tied there for who knows how long until one of us noticed," I say while I unclip her leash.

Setting her on the floor so she can roam, I shoot Emma a text asking if I can have some dog food. Next, I search for a blanket and something I can use as a water dish while the dog follows at my heels.

"You may not have had a dog before, but I think you have one now." Reese grins, crouching down and cooing at the pup. "What're you going to name it?"

"Her." The word comes quickly. Damn I just adopted this dog. Looking at her more closely, I realize how cute she is, and that she's not a puppy. Curious, I fill the bowl I've found and set it down. Grabbing the leash, I inspect it. Sure enough, written in sharpie on the leash is a name. Luna.

Clearly, she was a beloved pet to someone at some point.

"The leash says Luna. I'm going to go check by where I found her, something's not sitting right with me." I watch as

Reese sits on the floor and Luna wiggles over to her, her stubby tail wagging.

Turning, I make sure to close the door all the way. Once I get to the tree, I notice a camo bag in the dirt covered in some branches that must've fallen during the night. Now that I'm paying more attention, I notice the ground is wet. My heart aches for the dog, tied up sometime during the night and when there was a storm to boot.

Back in the shop, I show Reese the bag. She comes over, the dog—Luna—in her arms. Opening it there's a letter on top.

To the kind folks at Hyatt Ranch,

Making the decision to leave Luna tied to a tree marks the lowest point of my life. I have no choice and I couldn't face you to do it, so I took the coward's way. You see, I'm dying and I have no one to care for her. I was in the hospital for a week and the people who were supposed to take care of her forgot to feed her. I can't leave this world knowing she's not loved.

Please love her. She's 13 years old and she deserves to have a loving family until the end.

And please forgive me, Luna. Please forgive me for leaving this world before you and for tying you to a tree.

Forgive me.

Please love her.

Joan

Reese sniffles, hugging Luna closer to her.

"Why don't you keep her?" The words come out gruff. That letter damn near broke me.

She buries her face in Luna's fur, but shakes her head. When she looks up at me, her eyes are full of sadness and shame. "I can't afford her. I can barely afford myself and Sasha."

We stare at each other, her eyes glistening.

"Tell you what, she can be our shop dog. I will pay for her upkeep, but I think she should stay with you. She's used to living with a woman, it'll be more familiar to her." Petting Luna, the sadness in those brown eyes strikes me straight in the heart. "Your mom loves you. And we do too."

Reese sets her down with a visible reluctance. After loading the truck and ten minutes of promising the dog she'll be back, Reese is out the door to meet clients for the day.

"Let's see what Joan left for you." Cringing at the cooing tone of my voice, I clear my throat and proceed to empty the bag.

Dog bed. Food. Toys. Bones. Dog shampoo. Everything we could possibly need.

"You're here to stay, Luna. Let's go introduce you to the rest of the family."

CHAPTER TEN

Reese

The end of August brings cool mornings, which I love. Every morning I ride Sasha for an hour, Luna running alongside us, before heading to the shop or helping Dane with the horses he's training. Over the past month I've fallen into a routine and I'm happier than I've been in a long time.

Rubbing Sasha's nose, I rest my forehead against hers for a moment before picking up my tack. Luna follows on my heels as I close the gate and begin the short trek to my new tack space in the barn.

It's my first full weekend off and I don't really know what to do with myself. Dane and Emma have gone away for a week. Lia is prepping for a show with Alex frowning the entire time. And Ryan, well, he's moping because his doctor told him his arm needs to stay in the cast longer than originally thought. Probably because he uses it more than he should, he was bad from the start, but he got even worse when Luna came into our lives.

Smiling as I think back on that day, I remember how I returned to the shop to find Luna had met the entire family, been bathed, had a bed set up for her in the shop, and Ryan sat on the floor wrestling with her.

She's become a huge part of our day, coming with me wherever I go, and she even gets along with Emma's Doberman, Chloe. Girls' night got cancelled this month due to Emma's horse, Belle, passing away. It's one of the reasons they're away now.

I didn't realize how entrenched I'd started to become in their lives until they were all gone or busy. Closing up the barn, I try to figure out what I'm going to do with my day.

As Luna sniffs, running along a path, she starts up the trail that leads to the old, decrepit shed. I haven't been in there since my first day. Chewing on my lower lip, I remember Ryan telling me to make myself at home, that the bush around the apartment wasn't really used for anything, and the idea of cleaning it out and making a little "she-shed" makes me break out in goose bumps.

Pulling out my cell, I send Dane a quick text asking him if anyone is using the shed and if I can clean it up.

His response is quick.

> Dane: Go ahead, none of us has used it in years. I was thinking of tearing it down, but this sounds like a better idea.

Sending a quick thank you, I watch Luna zig-zag through the brush for a bit until my excitement gets the better of me.

Whistling, I wait while Luna comes bounding out of the bushes and we head into my apartment. My phone rings as I'm gathering things I think will be helpful in cleaning it up.

"Hey, Mimi," I answer, smiling when I see her face pop up on my screen.

"Hey! We just got back from camping and I wanted to check in." She barks an order at Sean, reminding me of last summer when we all went camping together. That's the only thing about this job that's not perfect, how far I am from them.

"Things are good. I have a few days off, so I'm just hanging out with Luna and we're going to clean out an old shed I found." Setting my stuff aside, I grab a water bottle and fill it up.

"That sounds—dirty—but you always did like to do things like that." I can picture Michelle crinkling her nose, especially at the idea of all the spiders I'll encounter.

"You know me." Laughing, I lean against the counter, my hand brushing the stack of envelopes I tossed there a few days ago. My stomach sinks, I've been avoiding opening them because I know they're all bills. Even with a couple paychecks under my belt, I'm still barely floating.

My sister talks about their trip and I respond in all the appropriate ways until we hang up. Setting my phone down, I look longingly at everything I need to clean out of the shed and back at the stack of bills.

Sighing, I meet Luna's eyes. "I guess I shouldn't avoid these any longer. The shed will have to wait."

Grabbing the envelopes, I sit down at the table and tear into the first one. The monthly loan statement for my lawyer fees. The big red stamp telling me I missed my payment last month taunts me as I take in the five-digit balance. Our divorce has been settled for over four years now, but the number has hardly gone down in that time.

With my bank app open, I pay the overdue bills first watching with a sinking stomach as every penny I made since starting this job depletes. I still have to pay Roy for paying off my truck and trailer. At least everything else is paid, even if a few are still a month behind.

Picking up my phone, I call him.

"Hey, darlin.'" His raspy voice makes me smile even as tears fill my eyes. He's stuck by my side through all of this and I will never fully be able to pay him back for everything he's done for me.

"Hi, Roy." My throat is tight, I hate being in this position.

"Okay, now someone as wonderful as you shouldn't be sounding so upset. What's wrong?" I hear a chain rattle, horses whinnying in the background.

"I'm so sorry to do this, but can I defer this month's payment to the end? Things are a little tight right now." No longer able to hold the tears back, they silently fall down my cheeks. The devastation at letting him down when he trusted me to follow through on my part of our contract pours out with each tear.

"Oh, Reese. Don't you worry about it. I'm not. I know you're good for it. If you remember, I didn't want you to start paying me back for five years. Now, focus on getting yourself a little more situated and take the rest of the year off from worrying about me." His generosity makes me cry even harder. He clears his throat. "Now you quit that."

"O-Okay. You have no idea how much I appreciate every-thing you've done for me." Tilting my head back, I breathe deeply.

We chat for a few moments before hanging up, tears still streaming down my face.

The spread of papers taunts me, but instead of succumbing to the temptation of a pity party, resolution fills me instead. Wiping my face dry, I sit up straight in my seat. I finally have a steady income, the Hyatt's are paying me a biweekly salary instead of per client, so I grab a notepad and start writing down my expenses.

Budgeting hasn't been a possibility until now and I'm determined to dig myself out of this hole.

Before I can finish, there's a knock on my door. Shuffling the bills all together, I shove them in my drawer of shame before answering the door.

Ryan smiles when he sees me, his big easy grin makes my stomach get all twisty in a way I didn't think was possible anymore. Not that I would ever admit it out loud. My little crush is my secret and something I'm going to get over.

"I'm done pouting." He waits for me to invite him in before coming to plop down at my kitchen table. I don't think he's used to his siblings being so unavailable.

Luna jumps on his lap, eager for head scratches.

"You know, an extra month in a cast is better than permanent damage." I turn my coffeepot on, turning in time to see him examining my expense list.

"You sound like my doctor—what's this?"

Snatching it away, I feel my face burn in humiliation. "It's nothing. Just a list. Not important."

"Reese."

When I finally meet his gaze, I don't see judgment, just concern. Sighing, I drop into a chair, my body sagging. "It's the list of bills I have to pay off. I was working on a budget when you knocked."

"You know, aside from learning to be a farrier, I also went to night school to gain a business degree. All three of us did. I minored in accounting so if you want help with your budget..." He scratches Luna behind the ears before setting her on the floor, planting his elbows on the table and leaning toward me. "C'mon, Reese. No judgment, just help."

Swallowing hard, I ponder his offer. I don't know him well,

and finances are an extremely personal thing, but budgeting is not my strength. I sit up straight in my chair, tear off the sheet I'd been working on, and hand him the pad of paper back. He looks at the paper then back at me.

"I don't feel comfortable sharing my personal expenses, but a budget template might be helpful." Folding the sheet I have clutched in my hand, I wait for him to argue with me.

He looks across the table at me and smirks. "I can do my best to show you how I like to break things down. Without knowing specifics, I don't know how much help it will be, but I understand your reservations." He pauses and glances across the table at me, his smirk widening into a huge grin. "You know, it would be easier if you were sitting next to me. I promise I showered today."

My lips twitch despite the heaviness I feel in my body and I shift my chair until we're sitting inches apart.

Over the next hour Ryan goes over how to build a basic budget that is flexible. He then lists anticipated expenses, something I didn't even think to do.

As we sit there, I find my eyes wandering to his face as he writes. The way he licks his lower lip when he's concentrating, his brow furrowed. And when he really needs to think, he stares off and you can practically see his brain working.

If someone would've asked me a month ago if I thought this is where we'd be, I would've said no. Ever since that day with Sandy, Ryan has been an incredible boss, and as we sit here I think maybe he's even a friend.

He sets the pen down, flexing his fingers. I notice for the first time that he looks uncomfortable and I realize he was writing with his bad arm.

"Crap, I guess I could've written."

"Nah, a little writing isn't going to cause permanent damage." He grins and shoves the paper toward me.

Scanning, I'm relieved to see that everything we went over is written down and I can easily take his template and add in my debts. I conceded and discussed my normal expenditures on myself and Sasha. As I scan it a second time, my heart sinks a little. "We didn't add a food budget."

"I know. Think of it as a perk. When we do our family shop you can come along and shop with us. We want our staff to be comfortable and happy. We've done the same for Nella." He taps the pad of paper. "All you need to do is input your numbers while following these principles and things should seem much more manageable."

"Thank you. I don't know what to say." I falter as I run my fingers over his hard work.

"Don't say anything, just fill it out and commit to following it. If you ever feel comfortable, we can go over your specifics and adjust it, I could even build you a spreadsheet." He stretches, his shoulders cracking. "I stopped by to see if you'd come to Linger with me. I need to get off the ranch, I don't think I can sit through another dinner listening to Alex fret over Lia. I'll go crazy." He shoves back from the chair, waiting.

Setting the paper down, I smile at him and hope he realizes just how grateful I am that he's here right now and that we're in this good place.

"Sounds fun. Just give me an hour to get ready."

CHAPTER ELEVEN

Ryan

As I pull up to Reese's apartment, I try to make sense of the funny twisting happening in my stomach as I shift into park and move to unbuckle my seat belt. I hope I'm not getting sick. Before I can open the door, I see movement from the corner of my eye. Snapping my belt back into place, I straighten in my seat and wait while she rounds the back of the truck.

When the door opens, I look over and smile at her, my greeting freezing when she hops in the truck and I get my first good look at her. Reese's hair falls in soft auburn waves over her shoulders. The floral dress she's wearing fits her curves perfectly. When she turns to smile at me, I notice she's done her makeup with a soft subtlety that highlights her already beautiful features.

I'm used to seeing Reese in jeans and button up shirts. Her hair tied up and usually free of makeup. On occasion her hair will be down, or she'll be wearing some other form of casual attire, but never all done up like she is now. I have to remind myself daily not to stare at her, that it's inappropriate to find my employee so attractive. Seeing her relaxed and ready to enjoy a night out reinforces the fact that my attraction to her just isn't going away. In fact, the more I get to know her and the amazing person she is, the harder it is to remind myself I don't want to like her as more than a friend.

My mouth feels full of cotton balls as I finally manage to utter, "Hey."

"Hey. You know, I'm excited to go out tonight. I can't remember the last time I was out with a friend." She falters over the word friend, her cheeks flushing, which just makes her even more stunning.

I wonder if the word is hard because she's still waiting for me to be an ass, or if it's because she likes me as much as I realize I like her.

Like is a funny word because I don't think it's truly appropriate for the heat flowing through me as I shift in my seat. Maybe this is a mistake.

Glancing over at her, I contemplate making an excuse to cancel, but I notice the weight she was carrying when we went over her budget is gone, and as she looks at me expectantly, her eyes are shining. I can't cancel on her because my hormones can't seem to stay in check.

Shifting into drive, I pull away from the safety of the ranch and the clear boundaries we have set here to head to Linger.

During the short drive Reese fills me in on Luna's antics of the day. We both love that little scruff of a dog and she's even started going with Reese to see clients.

"Finally, she stops rolling and she's green. Jesse mowed there earlier, and I guess it was damp and fresh enough that it dyed her fur!" Reese laughs, the low sound incredibly sexy.

Chuckling as I park the truck and shut it off, I glance over at her in the dark cab. She looks radiant. Swallowing, I hop out of the truck, heading to open her door.

Maybe it was a bad idea suggesting we go to Linger, with their low romantic lighting, and penchant for slow country songs. Being close to her is hard enough at home, but in a setting designed to set the mood, I'm in trouble.

The second she hops out of the truck, I realize just how much trouble I'm in. I didn't notice before the way the dress shows off her long, toned legs. Somehow, I didn't even notice the v-neckline showing off her cleavage. It's classy and sexy.

As we're walking, I try to keep my eyes on hers, not that it helps. Shaking my head, I remind myself that Reese is a forever kind of woman and I'm a for-a-night kind of guy. I would be lying if I said I didn't want what my siblings have, but the idea of being hurt, being made a fool of again, it's not something I'm willing to risk.

When I open the door for her, I notice that the dress is tied at the side. Swallowing hard, I chant "off-limits, off-limits, off-limits" in my head.

Reese's gasp as we enter the bar distracts me from my internal musings.

"Okay, I have to admit, the outside of this place doesn't do the inside justice." Reese gazes around the pub with its low lighting, cozy booths, and the signature glass-blown chandelier glimmering above the bar.

"Everyone always says that. The food is incredible and the atmosphere can't be beat. You also rarely have anyone other than locals in here because the outside looks so sketchy." Gazing around the bar, I don't see anyone I know. I don't know if I'm relieved by that or not. If Jesse or Ashton were here, they would create a decent buffer and maybe I could get these damn thoughts out of my head.

Settling into a booth, our server approaches and we order

our drinks. Reese gazes around us, taking everything in from the laughing groups of friends to the couples dancing to the country song playing over the speakers.

Our drinks are dropped off a few moments later and she turns to smile at me before taking a sip.

"I love this place." She looks around again, capturing every detail. When some guy catches her eye and winks, I scowl in his direction, but she doesn't even seem to notice because she's turning back to me. "There's something magical about it, everything seems to fall away, even just for a moment."

"When we go out, this is our spot." Taking a swig of my beer, I force myself to look away from her and scan the crowd. Grinning when I notice a couple arguing, I gesture toward them. "I think they missed the memo about letting things go in here."

Reese follows my gaze and watches as the guy turns to the bar while the woman turns her phone on herself, pushing her lips out. "Ugh."

"I hate that." We say at the same time, looking at each other and laughing.

"Who thought duck lips were a good idea?" Reese mimics the look but crosses her eyes and sticks out her tongue.

"Hold that pose, that's one for social media." Chuckling, I hold up my phone. Little does she know, I actually snap a picture because she looks adorable.

She flushes and looks down at the table. "How's your house coming along?"

"Slow, but that's probably because I'm getting anxious to move out of the main house. Lia's in her second trimester which triggers certain hormones that I don't need to be aware of. I'm contemplating moving down to the basement before I start having nightmares."

She laughs. "I've heard about the second trimester effect.

Apparently, it's the best sex you'll ever have." She laughs as I shudder. "Lia is an adorable pregnant woman, she carries it well."

"She does. And I can't wait to be an uncle. I started making the little bean a crib to surprise Lia and Alex." Waving his casted arm he says, "This thing has hindered me, but thankfully I have some time."

"Hold on, did you make the furniture in my apartment?" Reese leans forward, her eyes intent on mine.

"I did. It's something I like to do in my spare time, limited as that may be." It's one more thing I've been missing while being out of commission.

"It's absolutely beautiful! I love it all." Reese's compliment makes me sit up a little taller.

"Thank you. I usually make stuff to order, not a lot but enough to keep me busy, I've had to cancel on a few people and turn a few others away." Sighing, I scowl at my arm. I know in the grand scheme of things, the short time I'm wearing this cast is nothing, but right now it feels like an eternity.

"You hate feeling like you're not contributing."

Nodding, I pick at the label on my beer bottle.

"You know you're still integral to the business. Haven't you noticed how much your family defers to you about things happening around the ranch? Your opinion is valued. So even though you're not doing the physical stuff, you're still very much involved. And important." Reese's gaze is intent on mine, waiting until I give her a small smile.

"I guess I never thought of it like that. I thrive on being busy with my hands and my mind. I guess I need to value the mind part a little more."

She smiles at me and nods. It's amazing how much our dynamic has changed in a month. I never thought I'd be sitting across from her, confiding in her in this way. When I met her, I knew there was something about her, that draw I felt and wanted to pretend didn't exist, it's strengthening the more I get to know her.

"Did I tell you I met your mom the other day?" Reese intrudes on my thoughts with a little smirk.

"Please tell me she didn't tell you the story." Dropping my forehead to table, I groan. Of course, she told the story. She lives to tell that story.

"You mean the naked except your boots story? Or were you referring to getting caught with your pants down in the barn story?" Her voice is full of humor and when I lift my head up, I can see she's barely restraining her laughter.

"She's knows about the barn? I can't believe Dad would tell her that." Shaking my head, I chug back the rest of my beer. "At least the boots story is cute, I was four. The barn—not so much considering that was in this decade."

"I mean, I'd hope you wouldn't have been passed out drunk in the barn with your pants down and your hand—well, you know—when you were four." Reese finally can't hold her laughter back anymore, her eyes sparkling. "I just have one question for you, and I need an honest answer between us. You had a girl in there didn't you?"

Leaning back, I smirk. She's smart. "Yeah, I mean, I was drunk, but we heard the barn open and she scurried into a dark corner and hid. I pretended to be passed out. My hand was in my underwear to contain the situation. I was nineteen and stupid."

We both laugh. I was scared shitless that night. I was sure my dad would make me sleep it off in the barn. Instead, he told me to get in the house and after I was finished sneaking Rose out of the barn and to where her car was parked, I joined him in the kitchen where he'd made me some food and mixed up his hangover remedy. He asked how I got home, and then sat with me while I ate.

We talk for another hour as we finally order and eat. I learn about Reese's family and the amount of support they offered her during her divorce. Her parents couldn't afford to pay her divorce lawyer, but they co-signed the loan so she could hire a decent one.

By the time we've finished eating, we've been sitting in Linger for four hours. This time of night the music starts to slow down, and we watch as couples begin to flood the floor.

Reese sighs wistfully. "I miss that part of being in love. In the beginning, before Justin—well you know, he used to take me dancing every Friday night."

When she looks toward the crowd, her face has that faraway look that tells me she's not in this room right now. As I watch her soft expression of recollection, I realize that what I felt for Cece was a child's interpretation of love. It wasn't deep. It wasn't long-standing. But it did shape who I became.

If I'm perfectly honest, my pride was probably more hurt than my heart, but I haven't been able to see it until now. As I watch Reese watch the couples on the dance floor, I can see that she loved Justin and what she hoped their future would hold for them.

"It's crazy to love someone even when they start mistreating you. I was foolish enough to believe it was stress-related. That once the show season was done, he'd relax and realize his mistake. Except it just kept getting worse." Her voice is sad, her eyes trained on the couples before us.

The song ends and before I have time to talk myself out of it, I'm out of the booth and holding my hand out for hers.

"Come dance with me."

She doesn't say a word as her hand slides into mine,

holding on as I lead her to the dance floor. "Good to You" by Marianas Trench starts playing as I pull her into my arms.

She steps in close, the intoxicating smell of coconut and lime makes me breathe in a little deeper as we begin to dance.

The room fades away as she rests her head on my shoulder and the rest of the space between us disappears. She fits right into me, my arms holding her close as the song plays.

Closing my eyes, I imagine what I would be like if I hadn't let pride and hurt stop me from opening up to someone in the way I've found myself opening to Reese. The possibility of finding the happiness I envy in my siblings' relationships doesn't seem as terrifying as it once did.

Maybe my perspective has been changing ever since I saw Dane finally have a shot at the woman of his dreams. Or maybe it was when I saw Lia allow herself to trust Alex with her heart. That's all probably true, but I know seeing how strong Reese is, how she picked herself up when love screwed her over and knowing her heart is open to possibilities, has made me realize I need to grow up and stop making excuses to protect myself from being hurt.

Reese lifts her head, her eyes locking with mine. We don't say anything as the song plays out to the end, but I'm lost in her. And as we dance, I realize I don't want the song to end.

CHAPTER TWELVE

Reese

Setting my hair with hairspray, I shove a couple bangles over my wrist and grab my purse. I'm not sure what we're doing, but Lia tossed around the idea of leaving the ranch for girls' night.

I'm wearing new jeans with the narrow-braided belt Mom found at a local country store and bought as a gift for my last birthday. I saw it in my closet and felt bad for not wearing it yet. My burgundy top I'm wearing was an internet find. It's a unique empire waist style, the top part almost wrapped, the straps sheer. I loved it because of the round, gold-tone pendant with a neat maze design etched into the metal that's sewed into the shirt. I figured even if it was a bust, I could cut the pendant out.

I'm happy with the look. I haven't purchased new clothes for myself in a long time. After Ryan helped me with my budget last week, I used the pocket money he incorporated into it to indulge myself a little.

Smiling, I think about how much I've enjoyed spending time with him, especially after our night out. We walk Luna together every morning and ride for a half hour almost every evening after work.

It took until this week, but I've finally settled into a comfortable routine.

Luna prances at my feet as I slip into some strappy heels I found at a second-hand store. Patting her head, I give her an extra scratch as I apologize for going out. "I'm sorry, sweet girl. You need to stay here tonight."

Locking the door behind me, I start to walk to my truck when Ryan pulls up the driveway. He rolls down his window, hanging his arm out. When he smiles at me, I can't help the huge smile that crosses my face. My stomach flips a little as I walk over, wishing he was here to take me out.

My smile falters when I see a woman in his truck with him, my heart sinking.

"Have fun tonight! Stay out of trouble." He winks at me, unaware that the woman in the truck next to him is evaluating me.

"Just enough trouble to have fun," I manage to choke out.

He taps the side of his truck and drives away.

Shit. I'm falling for my boss.

My younger boss.

Not that age really matters, but I've gotten a sense that Ryan is nowhere near ready for a serious relationship and I have no interest in a fling, especially not with my employer. Stupid, stupid, Reese.

As I head to Lia's to meet the girls, I list all the reasons why I should shut down this crush.

He's my boss.

We barely just started getting along.

I know him well enough to know he's not interested in anything serious.

And, just because apparently my heart needs a reminder, he's my boss and is my make it or break it in this job.

I didn't think I was ready to start dating again, but listening to Emma talk about wedding plans, and seeing how much Lia's belly has grown over the last month, it's reminded me of everything I still want to have in my life.

I can't let fear of being hurt again stop me from moving forward. Maybe I should ask Lia about the local dating scene.

Once I'm at the main house, I let myself in and follow the sound of feminine voices. Lia is propped on the couch in their living room, her arms crossed and a resigned pout on her face.

"What's wrong?" My heart races. Michelle had a miscarriage before she got pregnant with Sean, everything had been going really well and then one night she had some minor discomfort. Before she realized something was wrong, it was too late.

"My hip is just bothering me, don't worry, baby is fine." Lia's voice is reassuring.

Relaxing, I sit down and try to focus on my newfound friends, but my mind keeps wandering back to Ryan. Not good.

"Why don't we make popcorn and watch a ridiculously sappy movie?" The suggestion is casual, but inside I'm scolding myself because I know the reason I want to hang out here is so I can see if Ryan brings that woman home with him. Maybe seeing him progressing their date will be the necessary kick I need to shut these butterflies down.

"I think that's a great idea." Emma speaks up when Lia opens her mouth to protest.

Twenty minutes later, we each have a bowl of popcorn on

our laps, we're all wearing comfortable clothes and since I ran home to change, I brought Luna back with me.

We watch the movie for a while before Lia turns the volume down. "Ryan has been really happy this week, like happier than I think I've ever seen him, I was wondering if maybe you have some dirt for me. You know, maybe some fuel for me to tease him." She grins at me conspiratorially.

Shrugging, I try to act nonchalant. "I'm not sure about all week, but when I was leaving the house earlier he was with some woman in his truck."

Emma and Lia exchange knowing looks, I know women enough to understand they know something I don't, but I don't know them enough to understand the words unspoken.

"Hmmm. That's not really unusual," Emma muses.

"At least, it was until recently. Ryan's been a bit of a home-body lately. Unusual, but he hasn't been pissy about it." Lia munches on some popcorn, grinning.

They're both looking at me like I should know more about it. I almost feel like a teenager again, but I remind myself I'm a grown ass woman. "Who knows. It doesn't really matter to me."

I make sure to hold eye contact so they believe me.

We finally return our focus to the movie, well, they do. My mind is circling. After Justin, I doubted I would experience the feeling of being attracted to a guy and doing something about it again. My divorce was a huge knock to my self-esteem, but I want to be that courageous woman who goes for what she wants again—except apparently who I want is my boss. That complicates things, more than I think I'm ready to cope with.

Emma and Lia break into laughter, so I laugh too and try to be more present. There's no use in overthinking this, nothing can happen. I have a plan, a good one. Pay off debt. Rebuild myself. Then find love.

Stick to the plan. Maybe I can incorporate some dating in there, without the expectation of it leading anywhere.

"I'm not tired, let's watch another!" Lia's bounces in her seat before wincing at the pain in her hip.

"I'm down. Reese?" Emma leans forward to grab the remote and starts scrolling through the movies available On Demand.

Luna sighs next to me, her eyes closed as she sleeps. I'm pretty cozy, and I would be lying to myself if I said I didn't want to stay longer to see what happens when Ryan comes home.

"Sounds fun!" I grin, promising myself to actually watch this movie.

As we restock our junk food, I bolster my courage before asking a question I never thought I would ask.

"Have either of you tried online dating?" My cheeks flush as they both swing around to stare at me. "I've been divorced for four years, separated for even longer. It might be nice to get out there a little more. Maybe meet someone."

Lia's grin is huge. "Well, Linger has a singles night every month. It's actually pretty good and most of the guys there aren't just looking for a quick lay. It's not online, but it's a good start."

Nodding, I snag a chip from the bowl I'm holding and munch on it. "Okay, thanks."

I flush again when they grin at me as we settle in for a new movie. This time I do focus since it's a romantic comedy I haven't seen before. The three of us are cracking up laughing when the door opens.

Inhaling deeply, I watch, only to sag when I see it's Alex coming in to give Lia a quick kiss and then leave again.

I need to get myself under control.

Sinking further down, I shift Luna so she's curled up against my stomach as I lay on the couch and get comfortable.

A door shuts, rousing me awake. I glance over and see that Lia and Emma are both fast asleep too. Blinking, I watch as Ryan and the woman come into the house. She's laughing, none too quietly. Sitting up, I flush as Ryan turns at my movement and sees me.

Lia and Emma sit up, stretching, and then Lia sees the woman next to Ryan.

"Olivia? Oh my God! I can't believe you're here! I thought you were in Croatia. Or was it Bulgaria?" Lia jumps up and runs to wrap her arms around Olivia who's laughing.

"Close, Turkey. I ran into Ryan and I wanted to come see you, but he insisted on taking me out to dinner first." Olivia grins, keeping one arm wrapped around Lia.

"This is Olivia, our cousin," Lia introduces us.

My body slumps into the couch. I was jealous of his cousin.

It was a late night, by the time my head hit the pillow it was close to three in the morning, but I still wake up with the sun. All night I was plagued with dreams of missed opportunities and it doesn't take a genius to figure out what my head is trying to tell me.

Instead of dealing with it, coming up with a solution, I dive into turning the rundown shed into the most amazing she-shed oasis ever.

Yesterday I didn't get very far. I cleared some of the brush encroaching on the shed. Loading my arms, Luna and I head down the trail that's starting to wear in the earth.

Pulling the door open, I start sorting through the mix and match stuff filling the space. Anything that looks like it could be meaningful, I toss in a box to sort later. The obvious trash is slowly filling up a garbage bag. Soon, the shed is completely stripped of everything.

As I clean it, my mind wanders to Ryan. It seems he's all I can think about.

Whenever I have something on my mind, I always over-think it until I come up with a solution, except this isn't the same as packing up and moving for a job. Said job could be in jeopardy because of this inconvenient crush.

It's not unheard of for people who work together to have solid relationships both inside and outside of work. Snorting. I can rationalize this all I want, but it comes down to a decision. Do I think these feelings are worth putting myself out there at the risk of my job security?

CHAPTER THIRTEEN

Ryan

It's hot as balls outside. Way too hot considering it's the first week of October. Not that I should be complaining, it could be snowing, but I wouldn't mind if it cooled off to a nice fall temperature.

For the first time since she started, I don't envy Reese working in this heat, I'm pretty sure it's the hottest day we've had since she started.

Thinking about Reese makes me smile. Her three-month probation is almost over and I can humbly admit Dane was right in hiring her. She's been amazing with clients and once I get this cast off next week we can start adding new clients to the roster.

The last month has been pretty incredible. I've never spent time with someone who makes me laugh the way she does. We've developed our own little routine and I thrive on it.

Yesterday we missed our evening ride and I didn't know what to do with myself, not spending that time with her.

Perking up when I hear tires on the drive, I open the shop door and watch as she parks. Her ponytail is a little limp, strands of curls plastered to her face, and her arms are coated in a layer of dirt.

She's still the most beautiful woman I've ever seen. Therein lies the only problem I've been having with her. The undeniable attraction that has become increasingly difficult to ignore.

"It's hotter than Satan's armpit out there." She groans as she lugs in her tools. Her cheeks are flushed, and her clothes are clinging to her body. At some point during the day she must have abandoned her usual flannel because she's wearing a tight tank top that hugs her curves.

"I have an idea. Go change into something more comfortable, I want to take you to one of my favorite places on the ranch. I can put your tools away, just be back here in five." I bite back a grin as she sighs.

"I can't shower in five. I need at least fifteen minutes." She stretches her arms above her head, her tank top lifting to show the smallest sliver of her toned stomach.

Swallowing hard, I look away for a second before meeting her gaze. "You don't need to shower. Trust me. Be back in five."

Five minutes later, she's standing outside the shop in tiny shorts and a sports bra. Maybe this wasn't such a great idea. Dane would kill me if he knew I was fighting an intense attraction to our employee. He would spout off about boundaries, sexual harassment lawsuits, and all that crap, like I'm completely unaware.

What makes it even harder is I'm positive Reese is attracted to me too. Every so often I see her watching me, but when I look at her she blushes and pretends to be focused on something else.

Clearing my throat, I point to the quad parked in the barn lean to. "Shall we?"

"I don't know how to drive that." Her eyes widen and she backs away a couple steps.

"Good thing I'm driving." Smirking, I arch a brow as she eyes my cast. "I can drive it, don't worry."

She sighs, slowly following me.

"Where are we going?" She finally smiles, her eyes lighting up a little.

"You'll see."

I hop on the quad, my heart racing a little as she swings her leg over behind me and scoots in close, her arms wrapping around my stomach. My abs flex a little when she accidentally tickles me, her voice a little breathless when she whispers, "Sorry."

Unable to formulate a response, I start the quad and race off, keeping my promise not to strain my arm.

Weaving through the trails, the wind blowing in our faces doesn't distract me from the way Reese's body feels against mine. I don't know how much longer we can pretend we're not attracted to each other.

The thing is, I need to decide if I'm ready to give something real a shot because that's what she deserves. Something real and long-lasting. Am I capable of that? It's a question I've been asking myself a lot lately.

We finally reach where the creek opens into a clear pond, the water crisp and clean. My body feels the loss of Reese's arms immediately as she hops down and kicks off her shoes and socks.

She's already ankle deep in the water before my feet hit the ground.

"The water feels amazing, and this spot is so gorgeous." She turns, her smile brilliant. "What a great idea."

The bank is mossy, soft on the feet. Even though the trees are changing due to cooler evenings, the water is the perfect temperature because of the hot day.

Reese sits on the edge, her legs submerged. Sitting next to her, I sigh as the cool water runs over my shins.

"Are you looking forward to getting your cast off next week?" Reese gently kicks her legs, creating little splashes, the tension she was carrying when she walked into the shop fading away almost as though the water is carrying it downstream.

"Yes. It's driving me crazy because it feels better but there is still so much I can't do because it gets in the way. I'm ready to go back to work too. The hardest part will be easing back in and rebuilding the muscle." Rotating my arm, I look over at Reese. "You're still planning on staying on, right?"

She nods, the affirmation sending a little thrill down my spine. "If you'll still have me."

I want to reply that I want her as more than my employee, but instead I say, "Definitely. I've never been so glad to be proven wrong."

Reese grins, leaning over to bump me. "At least you're man enough to admit when you're wrong."

Chuckling, I inch forward until more of my legs are submerged. I love swimming, but soaking in the cool water will have to be enough for today.

I watch in envy as Reese shoves off into the water, her expression one of complete bliss as she dips below the surface. Her tank top is practically glued to her when she pops back up, her eyes mischievous as she swims toward me.

Narrowing my eyes, I watch as she gets closer, her hands pulling her along the bottom of the shallows. When she pops onto her feet, her hand arcing over the water to splash me, I'm already lunging toward her.

My intent is to splash her back, but I throw myself off balance trying to protect my arm and end up tackling her into the water. Rolling onto my back, I quit trying to keep my cast dry and pull Reese up to the surface.

She's laughing and spluttering as she clings to me, our movements carrying us further into the center of the water. "Well, that's one way to retaliate."

"Full disclosure, I only meant to splash you back." My grin wavers as we stare at each other, her hands wrapped about my biceps as we stand in the deepest part of the water.

She lets go and pushes back away from me. "Since I'm staying, maybe I'll hit up that singles night at Linger Lia was telling me about."

My stomach sinks. I avoid that night like the plague, I don't want to give anyone false hope. The idea of her going and meeting someone is like a kick in the nuts.

Swimming toward her, I crouch low and look at her, searching her eyes. "Is that something you want? To go on dates with random guys?"

She flushes, her eye snapping a little. "They wouldn't be totally random. I'd talk with them, see if there was something between us, and go from there. Everyone is random in the beginning. I'm a thirty-four-year-old woman, Ryan, I want someone to go home to at night."

I want you to come home to me every night. The thought is immediate and fierce.

The intense need to pull her to me is strong. Instead, I wade closer. "How would you know who the right guy is?"

She swallows, her eyes dilating a little. "He would make me laugh."

Moving an inch closer I say, "I make you laugh. What else?"

Her eyes widen, flitting between mine. "We'd have to have similar interests."

Closing the gap a little more, I whisper, "We have similar interests. What else?"

Her eyes fall to my lips before flashing back to mine, her body quakes. "He'd have to make me feel safe."

We're only a few inches apart now, and when she licks her lips, my heart starts to race. If I cross this line, if she lets me, I need to be certain I'm worthy of her. She wants to feel safe, but can I do that for her?

As her eyes search mine, a feeling of intense protectiveness drives through me when I think of someone else being with her and potentially hurting her. Yes, I can do that for her.

"Do I make you feel safe?" My voice is a whisper as I intensely watch her.

She doesn't respond right away, my fingers itch to touch her, so I brush some hair off her cheek and tuck it behind her ear, my hand gently settles on the back of her neck.

Her eyes search mine as she inches closer until our lips are a breath apart, her hands falling onto my forearms. "Yes."

And then she waits, her grip firms, her breaths come in quick pants that tease my lips.

Tightening my grasp on the back of her neck, I close the distance and give in to my desperate need to feel her lips on mine. Kissing her with a fervor that shocks me, I moan as she presses her body into mine, deepening the kiss. It's not fast or hard, it's slow and exploratory. That burning attraction igniting. Running my hands down to her hips, I grunt in frustration when I can't lift her up, but she reads my mind and jumps, wrapping her legs around my waist.

I've never experienced a kiss like this, one that I feel in every cell of my body. My skin is cool from the water, but inside I'm burning up as I realize the difference between this kiss and every other one. The connection.

I'm not just attracted to Reese physically, but emotionally

and mentally as well. Something I hadn't even fully realized happened.

Running my good arm up her spine, I wrap her hair around my hand and tilt her head back as I trail kisses down her neck and over her shoulder. Despite my desire to explore her entire body, I capture her lips with mine again, the need to keep kissing her overwhelming every other.

Reese pulls away, dropping her forehead to mine and closing her eyes. We don't say anything as we catch our breath, so I wait until she finally opens her eyes and looks at me.

"Go with me to Emma and Dane's wedding." The words just fly out, but I have no interest in taking them back. I want to make plans with her, I want to dance with her all night. I want to kiss her again. For the first time since Cece, I want it all.

She takes a deep breath, biting into her lower lip before she nods. Releasing it, she leans down and brushes her lips across mine. "Okay."

CHAPTER FOURTEEN

Reese

My splurge items this paycheck was curtains and rods for the shed. It's been scrubbed, painted, and the double doors have been fixed. It's amazing what hard work has accomplished and I'm so excited to add some décor and a little day bed. Maybe make some cool shelves for one wall and create my own library.

My arms are full; lugging a stepladder, tools, and the bags with my new purchases as I walk the now well-worn path. Eventually I want to lay down slate stones and make it an offi-cial walkway.

Dropping them to the ground, I open the doors and move everything inside. I haven't seen Ryan since he dropped me off at my apartment yesterday evening, leaving me with a soft kiss. We didn't have any clients booked today, so I slept in before riding Sasha.

That kiss was the best kiss of my life. Hope fills me as I

think about where it could lead. Instead of dwelling on what I could lose, I choose to focus on what I may potentially gain. My forever.

It's doesn't take me long to get the curtains hung up, the pale green a soothing color that compliments the tongue and groove pine walls. The wood of the walls has been left alone, but I've been debating adding a pale stain to them to help protect the wood.

Dropping to the wooden floor, I look around with pride. The hardest part was cleaning every nook and cranny. There were cobwebs covering every surface, and because the doors were askew on the hinges, it took several days to get the mice out. That was fun, moving some old papers and discovering around six mice that all scurried toward me.

My cell rings disrupting the peaceful sounds of birds chirping in the branches of the trees surrounding me.

Glancing at the screen, I answer with a smile. "Hey, Mom. How're you and Dad doing?"

"We're well, we miss you though. When can you come up for a visit?" Mom's voice has this quality, even when I'm having the best day, hearing her voice just somehow makes it better. The woman doesn't have a mean bone in her body, and she always looks out for her girls.

"We're pretty busy until late November. Ryan's sister is getting married, so we've booked more clients than usual leading up because he's closing shop the week before and the week after the wedding." My stomach twists in excitement at going with him. I love weddings and I've heard some of the ideas Emma has been tossing around, it's going to be the perfect day.

"Why don't you come then?"

"Well, I'm actually invited and since I'm living on the ranch I thought it important to take part in the family activity. I want to stay here, and they really thrive on the inclusion of their employees, they even have a daily breakfast." It feels weird to keep the fact I'm going with Ryan from my mom, but I don't want her to read too much into it, especially since until yesterday nothing had happened between us.

"Well, I guess I should go, I just missed you. Oh, before I forget, Justin called here wanting to talk to you. I know his name is taboo, but I just thought you ought to know." Her voice is gentle, concerned.

"I'm not surprised, he's probably trying to get some final digs in before he moves south. Just block his number, I'm not playing his games." My tone is sharp and I can feel my face burning.

"Will do, sweetheart."

"Thanks, Mom. I love you." We say goodbye and hang up. Now he's harassing my parents, I'm starting to get pissed off because this is how it always goes. He pushes and pushes until I finally give in.

Enough is enough. Scrolling through my messages, I open up my string of texts from Michelle and send her the same request. Block Justin's number.

Sitting on the floor of my shed, I close my eyes and let myself think about our marriage. All the things I went through, the things I had to do to hide bruises. The daily whittling away at my self-esteem. The forced sex. The not forced sex. Shame starts in the pit of my stomach as tears build in my eyes, but I blink them away. I won't cry over it anymore.

Through it all, I remind myself I'm not to blame. It's not my fault. I'm worth more than that. I'm worth finding someone who loves me, cherishes me, and treats me with respect.

～

"She's moving so much better!" Grinning at Lia, I lope Sasha around the outdoor arena. "She's much softer and I can feel she's less tense. Thank you so much!"

Lia just grins at me as I work Sasha through some exercises.

After my call with Mom, I spent about thirty minutes reminding myself of my worth before I packed up my tools and cleaned my apartment. The entire time I was cleaning my mind circled around thoughts of everything that has happened in the last ten years.

I'm not where I thought I would be, but maybe life has a funny way of working out. I've never been as happy and content as I am now. Every morning I wake up eager to start my day. And now, I'm excited and nervous to see Ryan again after our amazing kiss.

If I hadn't married Justin, if I hadn't gone through everything I went through, would I be here today? Everyone always talks about things they'd change in their lives, but if we change things in our past then our present wouldn't be what it is. The idea of not being here, it's not something I care to think about.

Slowing Sasha to a trot, I cool her down a bit before hopping off and leading her out the gate Lia opens for me.

"Have you thought about breeding her? Her conformation is stunning." Lia reaches out to pat Sasha's neck, her eyes on me.

"I have, but I just can't afford the upkeep of two horses. The only reason I can afford her is because of your family's generosity." Tying Sasha up in a stall, I hold Lia's gaze, but she waves her hand.

"You're a part of the family now, you don't have to worry about her expenses." She smirks, her eyes dancing with mischief. "So, I know you keep things pretty close to the cuff, but rumor has it that Ryan is bringing you to Emma and Dane's wedding. Want to talk about that?"

I can feel my cheeks heat, but I just turn to Sasha and finish taking her tack off. "He is."

Walking away, I take my time putting her tack away before returning with a little less pink in my cheeks. Holding steady under Lia's scrutiny, I just shake my head. "Stop looking at me like that. Besides, I don't know what's going on, we haven't actually talked about it."

Lia grins at me, but before she can say anything else her phone rings, saving me, and she's waving goodbye as she rushes out the door answering it with a huge grin on her face.

The barn door opens again before slamming with a resounding bang. Turning, I bite back a smile when I see Ryan striding toward me. The look on his face is intense, my body heats as he looks me up and down.

He doesn't stop when he reaches me, closing the distance as he wraps his good arm around me, pushing me into the wall as his lips crush against mine. My entire body is on fire as he kisses me.

I guess yesterday wasn't a one-time thing. I don't think about everything I'm risking by allowing myself to explore this with him, I focus on the way I feel when I'm near him. Happy. Content.

When he rests his forehead against mine, I close my eyes and savor the way he holds me. No one has ever held me the way he does, he makes me feel cherished and safe, but also desired. Everything I want and deserve.

"I thought you'd never be done with Lia, she just doesn't know how to stop talking sometimes." He slides his hands to my arms, running them up and down over my bare skin. "I haven't been able to stop thinking about you all day."

"Neither have I." Pulling back, I open my eyes and hold his

gaze. "What is this, Ryan? I just, I don't want something meaningless, it works for some but not for me. I can feel that there's something here, I've felt it for a while, and I want to explore it, if you're interested."

He runs his hand through his hair, giving me a little half smile. "I don't know where this is going, I haven't even really thought about what it is, but I can tell you that it's not meaningless."

Huffing out a little laugh, I smooth my palms down my jeans and take a step back. "That's not really an answer."

"Okay." He takes a deep breath. "I want to be with you, I want to see where this goes, because I've never felt the way about anyone the way I feel about you. I'm not good with expressing myself or my feelings to anyone but family. I want to try. And I know you'll call me out on my shit when you need to. I want to explore this too. You scare me a little, but in a good way."

Laughing as he winks at me, I step back into his arms. "Okay. Now, all you need to do is tell Dane you're dating your employee."

He groans, but the smile on his face tells me he's planning on having fun poking the bear.

The barn door starts to slide open and Ryan moves to step out of my embrace, but I hold him in place. "I don't want to hide this. I'm thirty-four years old, I don't have time for games."

He plants a kiss on my forehead, taking my hand as we step into the aisle of the barn to see who just came in.

CHAPTER FIFTEEN

Ryan

I'm both relieved and disappointed when Alex comes sauntering toward us, his lips pulling into a smirk as he takes in our joined hands.

Now that Reese and I have decided to explore our attraction and see how it goes, I want to share it with my family. Partially because this will be the first time they meet someone I'm involved with, and partially because the sooner they know, the sooner they can get their opinions out and leave us alone.

"Have you seen Lia?" Alex doesn't say anything about our position, just goes straight to the point. I knew I liked him for a reason.

"She was here, but she got a phone call and left. She's not in her office?" Reese pulls her hand from mine to go and untie Sasha. Her face affectionate as she sneaks her a treat.

"No. Maybe she went to Nella's. I think she's hiding from me, apparently I'm too overbearing." Alex grins, completely unashamed as he waves, heading back outside in search of my sister.

"I don't think anyone else would ever get Lia the way he does. She can go a mile a minute and still have energy to talk your ear off." Shaking my head, it's hard not to see the difference having Alex in her life has made in Lia.

She's still the same caring person, but she's more grounded and sure. Both my siblings have found their person, the one that brings out their best qualities. It wasn't until I met Reese that I realized I want that too. It's shocking how easy it was to deny when everyone I met was missing a quality that I didn't even know I was searching for until I found it. It's also easy to see why I disliked her so much in the beginning, being around her made it tough to live in my denial.

Reese leads Sasha out to her corral, turning to me once the gate is closed and her halter is hung up. "So, how do you want to do this? Tell him together? Or are you going to do it on your own?"

She smirks as I groan. "You're not going to let this go, are you?"

"Nope, because I know what happens when people say they'll do something later. There's always a reason not to, until it all blows up." Her eyes flash with vulnerability, and I know this really has nothing to do with me.

Tugging her to me, I wrap my arms around her and rub the tip of my nose on hers. "When I say I'm going to do something, I promise it'll happen. However, I know you need to learn that, so we can go together and you can watch Dane's eyes get that squinty glare when he's displeased about something."

She swallows hard, her bravado faltering. "I hope he's not too displeased."

I know she's pondering the risk to her job, but I'm not

worried about that. Dane will be more concerned for her and whether I'll hurt her or not.

It doesn't take long to locate my brother, he's working a new colt in the training barn. His gaze is intent on the horse as he moves it over obstacles and introduces it to all sorts of stimulation. Reese and I sit on the bleachers to one side, my arm wrapping around her shoulders as we wait for him to finish.

Dane glances over when he sees us, his focus returning to the colt for a split second and then he double-takes back in our direction. Instead of the squinty glare I'm expecting, I swear his lips twitch in a smirk.

"I think we were worried for nothing, he looks fine to me," Reese teases as she leans forward to watch Dane work.

"Hmmm. I guess so." I'm skeptical, he must be up to something.

We watch for a while longer until Dane puts the colt away and leads Joy in. She's doing incredibly well and has so much potential, but we haven't found the right buyer for her yet. I glance over at Reese, watching the way her eyes light up as she stares at Joy.

"Reese, do you wanna ride her for me today?" Dane grins as she jumps up and practically vaults over the half wall into the arena. Dane hasn't even walked three steps and Reese is in the saddle and putting Joy through her warmup.

When my brother sits next to me, I give him a sideways glance. "Nothing to say?"

He snorts. "From the moment I met Reese, I knew if you were going to open your heart to someone, it would be her. There's just something about her, a quality I can't quite put my finger on, but she's your match."

Shit. Dane just pulled a Cupid on me. I can't even think of a response.

"Then why be all 'she's your employee' blah blah blah?" I can't help question.

Dane arches his brow at me. "Human nature, we want what we can't have. And you hate being told what to do."

My jaw drops and I turn to watch Reese as I process this before muttering, "This is just bizarre."

"Look, Reese was the most qualified person for the job. Best case scenario was that you'd become friends, but a little part of me hoped you would find what Emma and I have. Maybe it's mushy, probably all the wedding planning and vow writing, but you just don't seem as happy with the way things are like you used to be."

He's not wrong. I didn't realize it until Lia announced her pregnancy, but I want that. I want a woman to love and a family to cherish. I tried to deny it, and I probably would've continued to deny it if Reese hadn't managed to get under my skin.

"Well, hopefully this doesn't blow up in our faces," I joke.

"Don't fuck it up and it won't. Reese knows what she wants and she's not going to tolerate games."

We both smile as Reese leans forward in the saddle to hug Joy, her lips moving as she talks to her. "She's quite taken with that horse."

Dane stands up, watching them speculatively. "That horse seems quite taken with her as well. Maybe she's not meant to leave this property after all."

CHAPTER SIXTEEN

Reese

"Come in!" I apply a final swipe of mascara as Ryan shuts the door behind him, Luna prancing at his feet as he puts his shoes on the rack inside the door. Biting back a smile, I watch as he scoops Luna up and coos at her, his now cast free arm tucked under her. He's going to be an incredible uncle—which makes me curious if he wants kids or not.

"I'm pretty sure she would follow you home if I didn't keep her in the house," I tease as Luna licks his face and wriggles in his arms with such joy she's making it hard for him to hold her.

Ryan sets her on the floor with a final pet. He washes off her doggy kisses in the kitchen before coming to wrap his arms around me. Tilting my chin up, I meet his lips as he kisses me softly, slowly.

"Hey." His voice is husky as he lifts his head to look at me.

Smiling, I whisper it back before pulling his head down for another kiss. When we part, I'm feeling a little breathless and a whole lot giddy. I haven't felt this way in years. I honestly didn't think I would ever have this new relationship, excited feeling ever again.

"How does it feel to have that cast off?" I run my hands up and down his arms, reveling in the smooth muscles.

"Incredible. Now I can do this." He drops his hands to my hips and picks me up, holding me as I lean down to kiss him.

"Mmm, I approve."

The timer dings on the oven, so I drop my legs, reluctantly pulling away from him. Grabbing the oven mitts, I bend to remove the simple roast chicken, asparagus, and sweet potatoes out of the oven. I open my mouth to apologize for the simplicity of the meal, but I snap it shut. I know Ryan doesn't care and I know I don't need to apologize for cooking dinner, no matter how simple. Bending my head down, I quickly fill our plates as shame fills me at just how quickly that reflex kicked in.

"What just happened there?" Ryan comes up behind me, enfolding me into his chest and holding on tight. "You were being the woman I adore, teasing me and saying what's on your mind, and then you just shut down. I can see it written all over your face that something switched in your head."

Taking in a shaky breath, I set down the serving spoon I'm holding and turn in his arms. "I've always prided myself on being a strong woman, speaking my mind and standing up for myself. I lost a part of that in my marriage and I've been working hard to get it back. Sometimes I find myself getting ready to apologize for things I know I don't need to apologize for, like our meal. I guess that knee-jerk reaction to appease you before you could get mad kicked in."

Ryan stills, his head cocking to one side. "Darlin,' you could have made mac and cheese and I would be delighted. What we eat doesn't matter, what matters is that I get to enjoy dinner with you."

His voice is soft and reassuring, allowing me to relax a little more.

"I know. It's going to take some time, but I'm glad I have you with me to navigate this." My voice quivers a little, because the urge to apologize for this heaviness on our first official date is on the tip of my tongue.

"You just did it again. Let's clear one thing up, you never need to hold in your thoughts around me. Or apologize for an amazing meal, which I don't really understand because that looks delicious." He cups my cheek and tilts my head back. "I think we're beyond the idle chit chat stage of our lives. Let's just leap into the deep end."

Somehow, he knows and understands what's going on in my head. It fuels my confidence and I feel some of the trepidation fade away. It's amazing what a little affirmation does to a person.

Ryan gives me a gentle nudge toward the table and carries our loaded plates over. Once we're settled and eating, I find my curiosity burning as he talks about Emma and Dane's upcoming wedding.

"Is marriage something you want?" The question pops out and I can feel my face flush.

He sets his fork down and smirks at me. "I see we're jumping," he teases, before his expression becomes serious. "Marriage is something I avoided thinking about, until recently, but yeah, someday. What about you? I know some people get divorced and then never want to get married again."

"Not every marriage is bad, I just married the wrong person. Which I can't even regret because it led me here. So, yeah, I can see myself getting married again." His gaze is intense on mine as he processes that before he gives me the warmest smile.

"Good."

"What about kids?" He opened the floodgate of questions, the pertinent ones I need to know before this goes any further. I already wasted my time, I don't want to sacrifice any more if we're not on the same page.

This time he leans back in his chair, studying me. "I want kids. I think three or four."

My eyebrows shoot up. "Wow."

His face breaks into a breathtaking smile. "Does that scare you?"

I think about it for a minute. The idea of that many children doesn't scare me, but the fact that I'm thirty-four and we just started dating does. "The number, no. My age, yes."

He leans forward, reaching to take my hand, his eyes twinkling. "I'm not even going to comment on that because even if I compliment you, I'm sure it could be taken the wrong way. However, I'm not worried."

My entire body is thrumming as he runs his thumb over my skin. I'm pretty sure the look he's giving me has kickstarted my body into ovulating, even though I know it's not that time of the month.

Pulling my hand away, I clear my throat and resume eating before I throw myself across the table at him. It's been a long seven years. I felt so beaten down, I couldn't bring myself to let anyone close enough to be intimate with them until I focused on me. Now, I'm mentally ready and my body is screaming at me to give in to my physical need.

Ryan chuckles knowingly. If I've learned anything about him over the past couple months is that he's incredibly good at reading me. He always seems to know exactly what I need and right now is no different.

He picks up his cutlery and we both finish our meals in silence, the tension palpable as we steal glances at each other.

My palms are a little sweaty. When I look at Ryan, I want him so badly I ache, but there's a part of me that's scared to give more of myself to him, despite the brave front I try to put on.

I fall hard and fast when I let myself, and I've never been able to keep my emotions out of sex. The moment I open myself in such an intimate way, my heart is involved. And it's scary. I don't want to get my heart broken again and I know it would be even worse with Ryan. With Justin and I, we were in lust and jumped into marriage too fast. We connected on a physical level but there was always something missing and now that I've met Ryan I know what it is. We have things in common; interests, goals, values. The man I've gotten to know ticks off all the boxes on list for my ideal man, which means if it didn't work out I wouldn't just lose my job, my heart would shatter, and I don't know if I could recover from it.

Letting out a soft sigh, I realize I can't let fear of being hurt restrain me from finding happiness. I clear my past from my head and focus on the man before me. I need to trust my instincts, because I didn't with Justin, I know that now, and they don't lead me astray when I listen.

Standing, I bring my dishes to the sink, inhaling sharply when Ryan steps in behind me, caging me against the counter. His plate and utensils clatter in the stainless-steel sink as they land on top of my discarded dishes.

His breath is hot on my neck as he brushes my hair aside, his lips leaving a scorching trail down my neck and over my shoulder. His body is pressed against mine, every hard inch. Tilting my head to the side, my eyes fall closed as he kisses harder, more passionately, almost as though he's losing control.

I'm spun around, his lips crashing onto mine, his tongue seeking until I open to him. When his hands grip my hips and lift, I wrap my legs around his waist, grinding myself into him, moaning at the feel of his hard cock pressing into me, the friction of my lace panties so erotic I can feel myself throbbing with need.

Leaning away I say, "Bedroom."

That's all Ryan needs. His lips are back on mine as he strides into my room and lays me on the bed, kissing me until he pulls away and lifts his shirt over his head. Sitting up, I pull my tank off and toss it to the floor.

My heart pounds in my chest as he kisses down my neck before sucking one of my nipples into his mouth through the lace of my bra. Arching my back, I press into him, needy for release. He releases my nipple only to move to the other, until I can't take it anymore. I push him up and rip my bra off. Moving to my knees, I press him down and work his pants off. I appreciate the foreplay, but I'm about to combust.

His cock springs free as I inch his boxer briefs down. Looking up at him, I hold his gaze as I circle the head with my tongue before wrapping my lips around him and taking him all the way. I work his cock as I toss his boxers to the floor, only releasing him when he gasps my name.

Ryan's eyes are blazing, completely enraptured by me, and I've never felt so sexy or powerful as I position myself over him and slowly sink down. Throwing my head back, I start to move.

The feeling of his hands on my hips, holding me, guiding me, just adds to the incredible connection I feel forming between us. Slowing my pace, I lean forward and place my hands on either side of Ryan's head so I can kiss him, needing to connect with him at every point.

When I pull away, there's something in his expression that

I can't quite pinpoint, but it makes me move faster until I'm chasing my orgasm. I can't break myself away from his gaze as I clench around him, little whimpers escaping as I find my release. It's intense, my body shaking, my arms barely able to support myself.

Ryan flips me onto my back, pounding into me until he climaxes, his eyes holding mine the entire time with that intense gaze.

He lowers himself to my side, brushing my hair away from my face and cupping my cheek as he kisses me softly. "I knew you were dangerous the moment you introduced yourself, holding your hand out for me to shake for a solid two minutes. If there was ever a woman to break through my cold heart, I knew it would be you."

There's a hint of vulnerability in his eyes reminding me I'm not the only one opening myself up to hurt. I suppose that's a risk we both have decided we're willing to take and I will do my damnedest to ensure we don't regret it.

CHAPTER SEVENTEEN

Ryan

A bare thigh drapes over my waist, soft breath tickling my collarbone. This morning is the first time I've ever woken wrapped up in a woman I've slept with. Reese is tucked into my side, her arms holding me to her. I'm waiting for a little panic to set in, but it doesn't come. I don't feel even a single wiggling doubt. With Reese, I want it all and I want it now. Call me impulsive, but us Hyatt's tend to fall hard and fast.

Mom and Dad met, fell in love, and were married within eight weeks. Dane knew Emma was for him since he was like eight years old. Lia and Alex connected from the moment they laid eyes on each other, it took them a while to admit there was more, but once they did nothing stopped them from moving forward and embracing everything life tossed their way.

Opening my eyes, I gaze down at Reese. How did I think I could hold her at arm's length? Maybe I could have if I succeeded in bullying her to quit. Shame fills me at how I behaved. I know we've moved past it, but I never thought I'd stoop so low to try and get my way. I was so foolish.

Reese stirs, grinning at me when she sees me staring. "Creep."

Laughing, I lean down and kiss her. "I was just thinking about what an ass I was when we first met."

Her eyes practically dance as she rolls to her stomach and grins at me. "You know, I was thinking about that the other day too and as much as you pissed me off and were completely unprofessional"—she winks—"I think it actually helped me in a weird way. You fueled my anger and made me dig my heels in to try harder and prove you wrong."

"I was still an ass but thank you for forgiving me." Smiling, I stroke my hand up and down her back, enjoying the blissed out look on her face as she tries to curl in even closer to me.

We cuddle for a while longer before finally rolling out of bed around eight to get ready for the day. Now that my cast is off, I'm back to work. Under the advisement of my doctor I need to ease my way back in, so Reese and I will be going to clients together for the next month.

Funnily enough, today we're going to be seeing Sandy Johnstone.

It doesn't take long for us to be ready and on the road. This time is completely different than the first couple of times we worked together as we're laughing the entire way.

"I know it sounds petty, but I'm kind of looking forward to seeing Sandy today. It's like poetic justice to at least face one person who mistreated me and show her that she can try and run me down but I'm not going to let her hold that power over me. So many people I thought cared about me just cut me out, no explanation, no reason. They just disappeared. Suddenly they quit calling and quit replying. She's my opportunity to show the people of my old life, even my old self, that I'm okay." Her fingers drum on her leg, exposing her nerves.

Reaching across, I take her hand and squeeze. "I understand. Although, if I'm being honest, I was the person who cut people close to me out of my life because of pride and letting my anger get the best of me. I think some people aren't equipped to deal with things, not that it's an excuse."

I haven't told her about Cece, I don't see the point. Everything I felt and the way I let it rule my life, no one knows except me. It's my biggest shame and one I don't care to delve into.

When I pull into the Johnstone's yard, I see Sandy waiting with both her horses tied and ready to go. She doesn't smile as we get out of the truck, the only shift in her expression happens when I take Reese's hand. I'm not of the belief we need to keep our relationship separate from work, we are a family business and if all goes well, Reese will be a permanent part of my family.

"Good morning, Sandy." My voice is cheery. Now that I know more about her, I have to put on my professional face. There aren't many clients I dislike, but she's always been one I struggled with and after everything with Reese, well, let's just say that the only reason I haven't blasted her is because her husband is such a nice man. Granted, the guilt at knowing what she's done and not telling him eats away at me a little, but I don't have evidence to substantiate the claim and I honestly don't know him well enough to mention it. Besides, hopefully she's learned her lesson.

"Morning." Her voice is sullen, her eyes flitting everywhere but us.

Reese chuckles softly under her breath, her expression one of complete professionalism.

We each tackle a horse, so we're done in less than twenty

minutes, Sandy staying silent the entire time we work. Previously, she would talk my ear off about anything and everything. Today, we work in silence, Reese and I stealing amused glances at each other.

By the time we load the truck up and we're passing through their gates, less than thirty minutes has passed.

Reese bursts out laughing. "That was hilariously awkward. I'm not typically a petty person, but the look on her face was immensely satisfying."

"Sometimes it's hard to be gracious to people who've wronged you." Winking at her, I reach over to take her hand. We have a short drive to the next client's house. Thankfully, my arm is fine, aside from the muscles being tired from disuse.

"I like to believe I can rise above; I strive to be better, but in this case I'm allowing myself a little moment of smugness." She squeezes my hand, watching me as I drive. "How's your arm feeling? You looked a little tense toward the end of that trim."

Her voice is soft. Normally I would act defensive if someone questioned my ability to do my job, but I know that's not what she's doing. "The muscles just need to gain strength. I promise I won't overdo it."

The rest of the work day blurs by and I stay true to my word, I don't overdo it. My arm is smarting by the time our tools are put away, the muscles tired from working after so much time off.

Working alongside Reese today was a dream. I've always enjoyed the solitude of my job, but once we start booking splitting clients between us, I'm going to miss this. I loved being able to joke with her and sit beside her in the truck. I also loved seeing how much my clients have taken to her.

A few of them knew her from when she was married to

Justin, but they either didn't take stock in the rumors or they decided my backing her was enough.

It feels like so long ago when I was arguing with Dane over hiring her, when in reality we're just shy of three months in.

Seriously? I've only known her three months? It feels like so much longer. I find myself forgetting how brief it's been, but then again, she's so observant she seems to know more about me than anyone else, even my own siblings.

Reese comes over, wrapping her arms around my waist, smiling up at me. Those beautiful hazel eyes hold me captive. Some days, I don't know how to handle the connection with her, it's something I never thought I'd feel.

She lifts up onto her toes and kisses me. "We should go get ready if we're going to be on time for dinner at Linger."

Groaning, I pick her up and plant her on my desk. "Why did we agree to that again?"

Leaning down, I kiss her neck, smiling when she moans.

"Because Emma and Dane are getting married in less than a month and they're about to be insanely busy with planning. This is a pre-wedding shindig, so we can all spend time together." Her voice is breathless as she tries to stay focused, her body rubbing up on mine as I open a couple buttons on her shirt so I can expose her shoulder.

"Right. And we need to start getting ready right now?" Working a few more buttons, I push the shirt down until her black lacy bra is exposed. Kissing my way up her shoulder, along her collarbone, I pause right over her lips.

Cupping her breast, I rub my thumb over the lace, her nipple puckering as her breath comes in faster pants.

"We can be late." Her voice is throaty, her hands wrapping around my neck and pulling me to her.

In between kisses, we strip off the rest of our clothes, tossing them to the concrete floor of the shop. I should check that the door is locked, but Reese's hand grips my cock and strokes, distracting me.

Running my thumb over her clit, I relish in the sexy noises she makes as she works me harder until she's guiding me into her tight pussy.

Thrusting in, I capture her lips with mine, my hands gripping her hips as I pound into her. She clenches around me, her hips meeting every thrust as she murmurs for me to go harder and faster.

I barely notice a creak, when a voice says, "Are you guy—"

"Get out!" I pull away from Reese's lips to yell over my shoulder at Alex. The door slams behind him and we forget he was there.

Reese leans back on her elbows and I can't stop devouring her perfection as she cries out with her climax, my own following quickly.

Leaning down, I kiss her slowly, deeply. "You make me crazy."

She smiles, running her hand through my hair. "Good."

When we finally join my family—an hour and a half later—we're greeted with knowing looks and snickers.

"Nice of you to finally join us." Dane smirks, that knowing grin taunting me. I'm never going to live down the fact that he hired Reese knowing I would be attracted to her.

"Hey, they've beat Jesse and Ashton here," Emma defends us, sending an exaggerated wink in our direction.

"Seriously?" I look at Reese and wish I would've taken the extra time to draw another orgasm from of her. She insisted we leave since we were going to be the last ones here. "And you were worried we'd arrive last."

She elbows me gently, blushing a deep red as everyone laughs. I wait for her to slide into the booth next to Lia before following. All three women's heads bend together as they start discussing Emma's bridal shower. Since Lia can't go too crazy they decided to host a shower instead of a bachelorette party.

Alex and I have Dane's bachelor party all planned. He knows what day it is, but the activities are a surprise. The server comes to the table and I place a drink order for myself and Reese. Just past his shoulder, I notice Jesse and Ashton finally come in.

"Holy shit." I chuckle, leaning forward to tap the table and catch Dane's attention. Jerking my chin in their direction, I watch as his eyes widen, before a wide smirk spreads across his face.

Based on their dishevelled appearance, and the fact they're both sporting hickeys, it looks like Reese and I weren't the only ones late due to physical distraction.

Clearing my throat, the girls fall silent as they approach. Jesse is beet red. Ashton just looks immensely satisfied with himself. It's been no secret that the two of them have it bad for each other, so this outcome is of no surprise to any of us. What's a surprise is how damn long it took for them to give in.

"About damn time," Lia pronounces the minute they sit down, Ashton resting his arm along the back of the booth behind Jesse. It's so like her to say what everyone is thinking, I can't help but laugh.

"We're all thinking it," I tease when Jesse flushes even more.

Reese looks between us all humorously, she knows Jesse but hasn't met Ashton. I also don't think she knew Jesse is gay, but she leans forward to them. "Don't feel bad, Ryan and I were in your shoes before you showed up because Alex doesn't know how to knock. I'm pretty sure the vision of Ryan's ass is going to haunt him for a while."

We erupt in laughter, it's Alex's turn to look embarrassed and slightly green. "Thanks for the reminder."

The server returns with the drinks I ordered, before turning to Jesse and Ashton, relieving Alex of the taunts that were coming his way.

Lacing my fingers with Reese's I lean over and kiss her cheek. I honestly never thought I'd be here, happily with an amazing woman who my family adores. It never crossed my mind that I wasn't happy with my previous routine dalliances until I met her, and she challenged me in every way.

CHAPTER EIGHTEEN

Reese

"Hello?" Ryan's voice carries from the entrance of my apartment.

"In here." My voice is muffled as I step onto the last rung of the ladder to reach the box I stuffed up here when I first cleaned out the shed. I'd meant to bring it to Ryan sooner, but it completely slipped my mind.

"Please tell me you're naked." Ryan's voice gets louder as he crosses the room before appearing in the doorway. He smirks at me. "Is this a new prop?"

"Help me get this box down and we can discuss it," I quip. I'm not opposed to using the ladder, we could have some fun with it and Ryan loves figuring out ways to have sex on different surfaces. Desks. Counters. Fences. Saddle racks. He's insatiable and I love it. He makes me feel sexy and wanted.

Strong hands grip my hips and lift me down, he's up the

ladder, the box in his hands, and back on the floor within seconds.

"What is this? It's heavy." He sets it down on the foot of my bed.

"There's that old rundown shed over there. Dane had said I could clean it out, so I put stuff that seemed important in this box, and I've refinished the shed. Every pay check I buy something for it, I'm turning it into a 'she-shed.'" My voice fades off, Ryan's face paling as he stares down at the box.

He flips open the flaps, his face becoming stone as he sees the picture on the top. I honestly never looked too closely, but when he lifts it up I see that it's a picture of him in his early twenties if I was to hedge a guess, his arm wrapped around a woman.

His knuckles turn white as he clenches it in his fist, tossing it back into the box and closing the cardboard flaps violently.

"It's all garbage, you can throw it away." His tone is abrupt as he stalks out of my room.

Opening the box again, I look at the photo. The girl is smiling at the camera. Ryan is smiling at her. It's obvious he's crazy about her.

Taking a deep breath, I join him in the living room, sitting on his lap and pressing my forehead to his. "Talk to me."

"It's not important. The past is the past." He closes his eyes, trying to hide from me.

"The past shapes who we are and the choices we make. It's never truly gone. It lives inside us." Cupping his cheek, I wait. I can see whoever she is, is a touchy subject for him, but I know from experience that talking about the things that hurt us helps us let go of that pain and move into acceptance.

"I thought I was in love with her. We met, fell hard and fast —at least I did—and I was going to propose to her. I was crazy about Cece and she was using me, it broke my heart. She wasn't happy with the idea of a simple life, she wanted to be in the spotlight. She cheated on me with someone and now they're married." He leans into my palm, finally opening his eyes and looking at me.

My heart aches for him. He has revolved his life around work and his family. I'm all about keeping a close circle, I've been burned enough to understand why it's necessary, but Ryan has seemed closed off to outside relationships even once we moved past our rough beginning.

"You know, we all make stupid decisions when we're young. I married someone I barely knew, ignoring the warning signs about who he truly was as a person. Don't hold onto it and let it impact you this way. Learn from it, but don't let it rule your life." Running my hand through his hair, I try to keep my voice gentle and not too pressing, but I can tell this is weighing on him.

Ryan takes a deep breath before he gives a slight nod. "I know that now. I didn't realize how resentful I'd allowed myself to become until you."

"Do you still want me to throw the box away?" Wrapping my arms around him, I kiss his cheek.

"No. I'll take it and go through it." He tilts my head, pressing his lips against mine. What starts as a soft kiss, quickly becomes urgent. His voice is husky when he picks me up and says, "I think it's time we test out that ladder now."

An hour later we're sprawled out on my floor catching our breath.

"I think you need to let go of your anger toward yourself, young love blinds us. You need to forgive yourself. I know this because I had to." Running my fingertips over his abs, I watch him carefully.

"You're right." He sighs, his eyes softening as he gazes at me. His look is intense, carrying emotions I'm not ready to deal with, so I roll him onto his back, kissing his neck until he's ready for me.

CHAPTER NINETEEN

Ryan

Buttoning my shirt, I glance at the picture that used to be in my clubhouse. The same clubhouse that looks completely different now that Reese has turned it into her own oasis. I'm glad it's being put to use. I couldn't bring myself to go near it after things with Cece ended.

It was our spot to sneak around, she never was interested in being around my family and I was foolish enough not to question it. Reese was right though, I needed to forgive myself and I think staring at that photo allowed me to work through the feelings and settle on peace. I'm happy with where my life is heading, I'm crazy about Reese and I know she's my forever.

"Ryan! Are you ready? Even Dane is ready to go and it's his bachelor party!" Alex bangs on my door, laughter in his voice. I hear Dane calling from downstairs.

Grabbing the photo, I tear it up and throw it away. Releasing myself from my anger and hurt.

Pushing the leather of my belt through the loops of my jeans, I tuck my wallet in my back pocket and join them downstairs.

In one week my little brother is getting married. We promised Emma and Lia that we wouldn't maim him, which ruled out bull riding. Something we actually tossed around.

Instead, we're surprising him with snowmobiling and then dinner at the Fairmont Jasper Park Lodge. It's just the four of us guys, a close-knit outing where we can let loose and have fun.

Thankfully the cold spell from the first week of November seems to have passed and the middle of the month is shaping to be decent. Clear, sunny skies. A little frosty, but there is no wind and the temperature is cool, but not freezing.

Emma and Lia are already sitting in the living room snacking on trays of delicious looking treats. Reese steps in the door as I finish putting my boots on.

Wrapping her in my arms, I kiss her. "Have fun with whatever you do for a bridal shower."

She laughs. "Be safe."

The girls all know what we have planned for Dane, I'm pretty sure this is the only time Lia's been annoyed with her pregnancy because if she could, I think she'd be coming with us.

After five hours of snowmobiling, we settle into our hotel rooms and get ready for dinner. Dane's expression when we filled him in on what we were doing was better than we'd hoped and we all had a fantastic time racing along the trails.

I had to call the hotel in advance to find out what "resort casual" meant. Digging through my suitcase, I find the recommended polo shirt, a shirt I didn't even realize I had, and pull it over my head. I'm glad I made sure Emma packed Dane's bag so he didn't have to worry about it.

Checking my wallet, I meet Dane, Alex, and Jesse and we head to Moose's Nook Chophouse. Thanks to booking so far in advance, we have a table next to the fireplace.

Once drink orders are placed, I lean back and smile at Dane. "How're you feeling? One week until you're a married man."

"Dude, I would've married her last year if she would've let me." He grins, thanking the server when she sets his craft beer down next to him.

Lifting my glass I say, "I'm proud of you, little brother. You won the girl next door and you couldn't be more perfect for each other."

His eyes look a little glassy, so he tilts his glass up and takes a big drink, the rest of us grinning. I still can't believe how things worked out for them. I wasn't a believer in soul mates or fate until Emma and Dane, their love is enough to make me think I was wrong.

"So, big brother, I'm getting married. Lia's engaged and having a baby. What's in store for you and Reese?" Dane leans forward, eager to put me on the spot.

"I'm crazy about her. In fact, I'm positive I'm falling in love with her, but she's a little skittish about things moving too fast because of her first marriage. Once my house is done, I'm asking her to move in with me." Leaning back, I smirk at the shock on their faces. "People can change for the right person. Look at Lia and Alex. Prime example. Go from being fuck buddies to having a baby and planning their future."

Alex groans as Dane's expression changes to one of shock. "Yeah, we never told Dane about our friends with benefits agreement."

Chuckling, I watch my brother go through the stages of grief and disbelief. He's always looked at Lia with the sibling version of rose-colored glasses.

"I don't know how you missed it. I saw them sneaking off together all the time. I figured you knew," Jesse pipes in, smacking Dane on the back.

Before we can tease him more, the server comes back to take our food order. We all order the same thing, the pan roasted venison loin. My mouth is already watering and I'm starving, so I order two grilled shrimp cocktails to start.

Dane jumps in before we can resume talking about Lia and Alex's early arrangement. "Thank you, guys, for all your help and for arranging this awesome night. This next week is going to be intense as we get the one arena ready. Jesse will take care of the ranch while we finish building the temporary floor and get everything set up."

Lifting my hand, I cut him off. "No wedding business tonight, tonight's about relaxing and joking. Tomorrow we can worry about the ten-page checklist I saw on your fridge the other day."

Early the next morning we arrive back at the ranch, a little hungover and a lot exhausted, but ready to tackle the daunting task of prepping for the wedding. Before I dive in to a day of laying a plank floor over the sand in the arena, I head to Reese's.

Using the spare key, I sneak inside, shushing Luna when she barks at me. Thankfully, I trimmed her toenails this week, so as she prances at my feet her nails aren't making the tapping noises that used to accompany her every step.

Peering into Reese's room, I can't help but stare at her a moment. She's sound asleep, her arms wrapped around her pillow. Her long auburn hair is loose, laying wild around her, and I know she's my forever.

Glancing at the time, I silently groan when I see a text from Dane asking me where the hell I am. Sighing, I tiptoe in and kiss her forehead before sneaking back out.

CHAPTER TWENTY

Reese

Spraying my hair to secure the curls, I take a step back and examine myself in the mirror. Today is Emma and Dane's wedding day and I'm meeting Ryan's parents tonight.

The nude dress I bought for the occasion sits just below my knees in a loose A-line. The dress is soft, almost billowy, but it clings to me in all the right places. I love the slim-fitted, long sleeves, and modest neckline. Perfect for the occasion, but I still feel sexy when I spin and check out the fit of the exposed back.

My slight tan from the summer has faded, but I still have some freckles that are stubbornly sticking around. Ryan loves counting my freckles.

Twisting this way and that, I finally turn away from the mirror and take a deep breath. I really want Ryan's parents to like me, I'm crazy about him and this is a step that I know is important to him. He's been asking me about meeting my family for the last few days. Something shifted after he went out with the guys, almost as though watching his younger brother get married has made him realize he wants more and he wants it now.

Wrapping a gorgeous, deep green shawl over my shoulders, I choose to walk to the arena instead of drive. The trails leading to the barn are lit by rustic lanterns, the flames of the tall pillar candles flickering creating a romantic atmosphere. Wrapped around the top of the lanterns are red carnations, red roses, white poppies, white roses, and sprigs of baby blue eucalyptus. All of them were hand done. Outside the arena, evergreen boughs drape over the wide-open barn doors. Larger versions of the trail lanterns line the wide walkway illuminating the pathway to the doors.

Standing outside, I spot Ryan talking and laughing with a couple I immediately know are his parents. People filter in and out of the arena around them. I smile and wave at the people I recognize, before straightening my shoulders and approaching Ryan.

The smile he greets me with is a combination of happiness and lust, it makes my heart flutter and my core clench at the same time. He strides over to me, wrapping his arms around me and kissing me without holding back. When he finally lets me go, I know my face is flushed even more than it was from the cool air.

"Reese, these are my parents, Juliette and Darren." He keeps his arm wrapped around me as I shake their hands.

"It's wonderful to finally meet you. I've been begging Ryan to bring you over for dinner, but there's a reason they encouraged us to build our retirement home on the opposite side of the property." Juliette's grin is one hundred percent mischievous as she feigns being heartbroken.

"Get the poor woman inside, Ryan. You must be freezing

standing out here," Darren admonishes, and I immediately know where Ryan inherited his protective streak.

We step inside the barn, my gasp audible as I finally take in everything they've done.

The sand is covered with a wood plank floor that's so gorgeous, you'd have no idea it was just installed this week. Wooden chairs fill the space on either side of the aisle and a chalkboard announces that there is no seating plan for the evening.

Ryan leads me to the spot he saved for me, a row behind the wedding party. In the front row are three seats, each containing a photo and a small bouquet of flowers.

"One for her dad, mom, and grandfather," Ryan explains as I sit down.

He leans over, kissing me softly.

"I need to go finish getting ready. You're sitting next to me at dinner, the head table is the only one with a seating plan and Emma wanted you there with me." Nodding, I get comfortable, watching as the seats fill up.

The arena looks magical. The tiniest string lights criss-cross the tulle covered ceiling and the walls have sections where thin twine is hung and small wooden clothespins hold pictures of Emma and Dane as children, together and separately. A life that's led to this point.

Music starts as the justice of the peace takes her place at the front of the room, letting us know the ceremony is about to start, and soon the remainder of the chairs are occupied. Next, Dane, Ryan, and Jesse stand at the front of the room, Ryan winking at me from his place next to Dane.

"Good to You" by Marianas Trench starts playing, and everyone turns to look. Lia leads the way, her burgundy dress complimenting her dark hair and the adorable baby bump. I smile to myself thinking back to the night I danced with Ryan to this same song as I watch Lia walk to the front of the room.

We all stand as Alex starts to walk Emma down the aisle. She looks absolutely stunning, the floor length gown simple and elegant. The capped sleeves and sweetheart neckline compliment her frame to perfection. The lace overlay adds detail but doesn't make the dress too busy. No one can take their eyes off her as she makes her way toward Dane.

The entire ceremony, I can't help the tears that fill my eyes as they stare at each other in complete adoration. If I found someone who looked at me the way Dane does Emma, I wouldn't hesitate to marry again.

Glancing over at Ryan, our eyes lock and my heart begins to race. He's not paying attention to what's happening, he's entirely focused on me and he has that look. The same look of adoration and love. The one I've always wanted.

How did I miss the fact he's fallen for me? Even more curious, how did I miss the fact that I feel the same? My heart pounds, the urge to leap up and race into his arms is overwhelming. I don't want to keep this inside. I promised myself when we started this relationship I wouldn't hold back, and I intend to keep that promise.

Jesse nudges Ryan when it's time for him to give Dane the ring, Ryan missing the cue, and I tear myself away to watch them say their vows.

Once the ceremony is done, the bridal party is whisked away for photos, so I rush home to let Luna out before the reception begins. Family and friends help rearrange the barn so there's a dance floor in the center of the tables.

By the time I return, it's been transformed once again. The rustic style of the decorations is perfection, everything laid out so precisely and with such care. I'm sure Emma and Dane are going to be thrilled with the outcome.

Strong arms wrap around me and hold me close. "I couldn't stop looking at you the entire time. You look gorgeous. I can't wait to dance with you all night and then strip you out of your dress later."

Smiling at the deep, husky tone of Ryan's voice, I turn in his arms to kiss him. When I pull away, I intend to tell him how I feel, but the words won't come out. Fear pits itself into my stomach, telling me it's too soon and I should've learned my lesson from being too impulsive.

Burying my face in Ryan's shoulder, I swallow hard and tell that fear to go fuck itself. The difference between then and now is the look on Ryan's face when he's looking at me. Ryan looks at me with affection, attraction, and love. Pulling back, I gaze into Ryan's eyes, wrapping my arms around his neck. "I love you."

His smile is immediate as he leans down, kissing me gently. "I love you, too."

He leads me to the head table, pulling my chair out for me. Cheers draw our attention and we turn to see Dane and Emma sauntering in. They're glowing as they slowly make their way through the crowd, stopping to talk to people on their way.

Once everyone is seated, Ryan stands up and heads down to the podium.

"Hey, everyone. I'm going to keep this short and uncharacteristically sweet, so pay attention. Dane, not only am I so proud of you for knowing Emma is the woman for you, but also diving in and going for it. You didn't allow anything to stand in your way. I admire you and your willingness to share your heart, and you're an inspiration to me. Congrats, Dane and Emma, I know you have a long and happy road ahead of you!" Ryan's smile reaches his eyes as he looks at Dane and Emma, lifting his glass and taking a drink of his champagne.

Later that night, we're two-stepping along to "Flatliner" by

Cole Swindell and Dierks Bentley, his words flash through my mind every time he smiles at me. I want to be the woman who jumps in, saying to hell with fear and believing in my heart. It may not always pay off, but as the song changes to a slow one and Ryan pulls me into his arms, I'm pretty sure I've hit the jackpot.

CHAPTER TWENTY-ONE

Ryan

Chloe jumps up when I enter the kitchen, only to drop her head and lay back down when she sees it's only me. Emma and Dane have been gone for a week and a half now, and I've never seen a dog so put out from being separated from her person.

"I'm trying not to take her reaction to me every morning personally, but damn, being snubbed by one of the friendliest dogs in the world is starting to hurt." I chuckle, joining Lia at the counter.

She smiles at me, adding some more strawberries to the fruit platter she's prepping. "She's never been separated from Emma before, but I know what you mean. She refuses to sleep in our room. In the morning, she sits on the couch, facing the window. Not that you would know." Her voice is teasing. Smirking, I reach out to ruffle her hair.

"Yeah, well, it's nice not having to put headphones on every night," I shoot back, laughing when she blushes.

"Besides, sleeping next to Reese, even in that puny queen size bed, is better than being alone in my bed."

Lia hands me some tomatoes to cut, her lips pursed in thought. "I really like Reese. She's sweet and grounded. I really hope she's here to stay."

"If I have any say, she is."

"Good. Mom and Dad really like her too. They said they had a chance to talk to her a few times at the wedding. Mom's already fantasizing about helping with more grandchildren." Lia runs her hand over her stomach. Every day it looks a little bigger, which Lia jokes about constantly. I've never seen my sister so calm and content.

I really believe it's true, when we find the perfect person for us, they bring out our best qualities.

～

"I can't believe they locked me out of my own damn house." Trying the knob again, I turn to Reese in time to see her press her lips together to fight a smile. "It's not funny! How am I supposed to know whether they're doing it right?"

"You're supposed to trust the person you hired. Besides, it's to protect you from having anyone who happens to wander down here from walking into your house." Reese comes up the steps and takes my hand. "C'mon. The wind is cutting through my sweater and I really want a cup of hot chocolate. Let's go back to the main house, light a fire and watch a movie. I'm sure Lia and Alex would join us."

Grumbling, I take her hand and follow her back off my porch, slowly walking to where I parked around to the side of the house. I just wanted to show her the progress inside the house. Especially the room I thought she could turn into a library. Ever since she found out Emma is an author, she's been devouring her books and anything else Lia and Emma recommend. I still haven't asked her to move in with me, but I was planning on it when I showed her the front room. Then I was going to ask for her input on shelving so I could hire someone to build and install custom shelves to her specifications.

Reese's hair moves as another gust hits us, her cheeks rosy from standing outside. Even though there's still no snow on the ground, the wind has made it feel cooler than it actually is. Surprisingly, the leaves are clinging to the trees, despite the mid-November wind. It's rare to still be surrounded by the bright oranges, yellows, and reds at this time of year. The colors create a beautiful backdrop around my house, complementing the red shade I chose. The exterior work has been complete for about a month now and they're making substantial progress on the inside. This time next year, we can sit in our house by the fireplace and watch a movie on our tv.

As we're heading to the truck, a white pickup pulls into the build-site. We're parked around the corner, they have no clue that we're here. Squinting my eyes, I try to make out the driver. I don't recognize the vehicle and the sun is glinting off the windshield making it impossible to see inside.

My guard is up as soon as I see the doors open.

"Stay here." My voice is low. There has been a significant increase in thefts occurring in the area and one of my neighbors said they suspected the culprits are armed.

Reese chuckles. "Ryan, it's okay."

"No, what if they're armed and they hurt you? I couldn't take it." Turning, I gently hold onto her biceps. "Please."

"I truly appreciate your concern, but that's my parents' vehicle. I guarantee they're not armed, and they never hurt me in my life, so I doubt today will be any different." She smiles, her eyes shining with amusement.

The tension in my shoulders disappears as I turn to see a couple bickering, their arms waving in the air.

Reese steps around me. "What're you guys doing here?"

She closes the distance, hugging them both. I trail closely behind, laughing at myself. Maybe Dane was right, we should probably install gates and a security system. I was about to tackle her father.

"Well, you've been too busy to visit us, so we came to you. Plus, we wanted to meet your fella." Reese's father's voice is raspy and deep, I can imagine it's intimidating when he's angry, but the laugh lines around his eyes tell me that doesn't happen often.

"Right. Sorry, Mom and Dad, this is Ryan. Ryan, my parents Joseph and Colleen."

We shake hands, getting the typical greetings out of the way.

"This is a mighty fine house. The nice young lady at the other entrance pointed us in this direction. When do you expect to move in?"

Joseph listens with interest, following me around the house as I fill him in on the schedule and point out different features.

"This is a family sort of house." Colleen's voice is a little suggestive, the smile on her face brilliant as she looks between Reese and me.

Reese shakes her head, smiling as she rolls her eyes. "C'mon, Mom. It's a little soon to be talking about family."

Looking between her parents, I turn to her with a smirk. "Is it?"

Reese's eyes widen as her parents grin even more. Her cheeks reddening more than they already were and this time it's not from the cold.

"I like this young man, Reese," Joseph approves.

Taking Reese's hand, I squeeze gently before distracting her parents with more information about what I plan on doing around the house, including the landscaping to add privacy from the customers travelling to Lia's clinic.

When Reese starts shivering, I invite her parents to stay for dinner. The comment about not being too soon to talk about family started as a joke, but as the four of us head to the main house in her parents' truck, I can't help but wonder if the timing is perfect.

CHAPTER TWENTY-TWO

February

Reese

I'm startled awake by Ryan's phone ringing. Nudging him, I reach for mine and immediately sit up when I see it's four o'clock in the morning.

"Ryan! Someone's calling you at four am, you need to answer." Leaning over him when he just grunts and rolls over, I see it's Lia calling.

"Lia! Is everything okay?" I try to calm my voice, shaking Ryan awake as I answer.

"Everything is fine. I just wanted to let you know we're headed to the hospital. I started feeling some contractions and Alex wants to head there now so we make sure we arrive on time. I told him they're still too far apart, but he's insisting."

Lia's voice is chipper, but I can hear Alex in the background saying five minutes apart is not too soon.

Laughing, I point to the phone and mouth, "Lia's in labor" when Ryan finally sits up. "Okay, we'll head out soon."

"No rush, it could take a while." Lia pants, Alex encouraging her to breathe in the background.

"We don't want to miss this."

Hanging up, I hop out of bed rushing throughout my room to get dressed. My stomach kind of hurts, it hurt a little when we crawled into bed four hours ago, but I ignore it as I brush my teeth. I will grab some antacids before we leave.

Ryan's texting Jesse and the rest of his family as he finishes getting himself dressed and letting Luna out.

Within twenty minutes we're on the road. Ryan's focus intent on the dark road the entire drive into town, watching for deer and moose.

"Do you want to stop and grab a bite to eat before we head to the hospital?" He finally glances over when we hit the edge of town.

"No, I'm too excited to eat." My stomach still hurts and I'm not hungry.

"Are you sure? I need to eat, I'm starving. Maybe something for later?" Ryan signals and maneuvers his way into the donut shop drive through, a lone vehicle ahead of us.

I'm about to shake my head, but it's a smart idea. We'll be at the hospital for a while and I'm sure eventually I'll be hungry and grateful Ryan had the sense to suggest we get food.

"Yeah, maybe we can bring in a box of muffins for everyone to eat and I can have one of those later."

He orders quickly, passing the muffins and his breakfast croissant over to me to hold, while putting a coffee into the console.

Once we're at the hospital, it takes a wrong turn and asks for directions to finally find the waiting room where the rest of the family awaits. Everyone looks a little tired, but excitement outweighs the exhaustion from the early hour.

"Any word?" Ryan sets the box of muffins on the table, taking the seat next to me.

"She's moving along, but not in active labor yet," Juliette fills us in, reaching out for a muffin. "Thanks, hon. This was a great idea."

"It was Reese's." Ryan smiles, taking my hand with his free one while he eats with the other.

Things between us have been going incredibly well, he even asked me to move in with him once the house is finished. Our families have met and I've never felt so happy in my entire life. It's been a dream.

We've argued, and made up, a few times. Especially when someone broke into the shop and I refused to move into the main house. Within two days, gates were installed on all ranch entrances and an extensive alarm system followed a week later.

Smiling, I think back to making up after that fight.

A few hours pass and Lia's moved into active labor; the entire room is on pins and needles as we wait for the big moment.

My stomach is killing me even more, I'm nauseous and sweating.

"I'm going to run to the washroom. Be right back." I kiss Ryan on the cheek and slowly walk out to the hall. I don't want him to worry, it's probably just something I ate yesterday, but I'm about ready to throw up.

Clutching my hands to my stomach, I heave when I get inside the stall. I don't even have time to close the door. My stomach is empty though and the pain radiating into my right side is difficult to ignore. Why, oh why does stomach pain always hit at the worst time?

Another stall opens, but I'm feeling too awful to care.

"Are you okay, dear?" a kind voice asks from behind me.

"Not really." Straightening, I turn and come face-to-face with a nurse. Her expression is concerned as she takes in my hands clutched to my right side.

"May I ask what's wrong?"

"Last night my stomach started to hurt." I wave my hands in front of where it started. "And it's just getting worse. It hurts to touch and I'm super nauseous. Maybe if I ate it would help, but I'm just not hungry."

Her face morphs, instantly becoming serious. "I think we need to get you seen by a doctor."

I nod, rising to stand and follow her down the hall toward the emergency room. Fear rushes through my veins when I hear her murmur something about testing for appendicitis. With a quivering hand, I send Ryan a text explaining where I am and what's going on and promise I will keep him posted. I followed up with a "Please don't worry and focus on Lia. Give her my best." text before dropping my phone back into my purse.

The nurse rushes me right into an exam room after my information is taken. The doctor confirms the nurse's hypothesis and they give me some IV fluids and antibiotics, while explaining the procedure for an appendectomy.

Once the antibiotics are in my system, I'm wheeled into surgery.

My nerves kick up as the general anesthesia is administered. I've never had surgery before, so even though I know it's a simple one I can't help but wish Ryan was with me. The world becomes blurry, my nerves dissipating as the anesthesia takes effect.

By the time I wake up, I'm settled in a hospital bed. The curtain slides to the side and the nurse who diagnosed my symptoms appears, that same kind smile on her face.

"Hello, dear. I'm glad to see you're awake. The doctor is going to be in shortly to chat, but I wanted to check in on you myself." Something flickers in her face, it's quickly gone as she checks my vitals, chatting away while the only thing I can think about is Ryan.

"I'm surprised your family isn't here yet." Her voice is gentle, but there is a hint of judgment that makes me jump to Ryan's defense.

"My boyfriend is here, his sister was in labor when I left, so he's probably still there." My tone is sharp, and I immediately feel guilty. "Sorry, I just hate that I'm missing it."

She finally finishes and after handing me my purse, she leaves me to eagerly check my phone. Two failed to send messages and nothing else. I try to send a new text, not wanting to disturb the patient snoring softly on the other side of the curtain.

The bar moves across before the alert comes to tell me it failed to send. Groaning in frustration, I'm about to open my settings when the curtain slides back, this time a doctor stands on the other side.

"How are you feeling, Miss McMillan?" He picks up my chart and jots a couple notes, before meeting my gaze. Something feels off.

"Okay, I suppose." Overall, I do feel better. At least the severe pain in my stomach is gone, thanks to the pain meds. As soon as I get through to Ryan, I'll feel much better. He must be so worried.

"The appendectomy went well. In a few hours, the nurses will help you get up and move around. In two to three weeks you can return to normal activities." He continues talking about things to watch out for, signs of infection and other possible complications.

He's in and out quickly, his manner to the point.

I'm sure he's extremely busy, but compared to the kind nurse, his brusque attitude is abrasive.

About twenty minutes after he leaves, my abdomen starts cramping and I feel a flood of warmth between my legs. My heart starts to pound as I lift the blanket and notice blood.

Bile rises in my throat, as I hit the call button. *This isn't normal.*

The nurse comes rushing in, her face concerned when she notices me shaking.

"What's wrong, dear?" Her eyes scan the equipment, efficient in her perusal.

"I'm bleeding," I manage to choke out as I lift the covers.

Everything starts to blur as I'm examined and cleaned up.

The doctor from earlier sits on a stool, wheeling closer to me.

"Reese, when was the last time you had your menstrual cycle?" His voice is gentle, a complete one-eighty from earlier.

Pulling out my phone, I check my tracker app. The date glares up at me, mentally counting back, I whisper, "Eight weeks ago."

He nods, not surprised. He starts talking, words like "miscarriage" and "common occurrence" blaring out at me over the ringing in my ears.

My throat feels like it's closing, the crushing devastation hitting me with each word.

"I suggest you make an appointment with your primary physician, I notice it's been a while since you've had a full exam. If you and your partner are trying to have a baby, it's always wise to get checked out. We recommend a yearly exam, regardless." He asks if I have any questions and I mutely shake my head, barely managing to utter a thank you before he leaves.

CHAPTER TWENTY-THREE

Ryan

When twenty minutes pass with Reese being gone, I become a little worried.

An hour and my worry becomes extremely concerned.

Multiple texts, a few hours, and the arrival of my niece, Stella, my concern turns to hurt and anger. How could she disappear during this time, without even a text or call? This event is so important, we'd been talking about it for weeks. I try to tell myself she has a good reason to have disappeared, that something must have come up, but how can she disappear without sending a message to explain why?

You would think that in an emergency, she would be able to reach out.

Returning from the cafeteria for the second time, I give Dad my cell phone before letting myself into Lia's hospital room. If I wasn't so angry, the scene that greets me would be amusing. Stella is asleep in her arms. Lia looks exhausted, but she's glowing as she hums and stares at Stella. Alex is passed out, snoring loudly, hanging halfway off his chair.

"Where's Reese?" Lia's voice is soft as she looks away from her precious daughter to me, tilting her head to see if Reese is behind me.

"I have no idea." I try to disguise my anger, but Lia sees right through me. I can't even lie, because there's no excuse for her to not be here without at least providing a reason.

Her face falls. "Oh."

"I'm so sorry, Lia. I never expected this from her. I'm reeling. I don't know what the hell happened. She left to go to the bathroom and never came back. My calls go straight to voicemail. I've left messages and sent several texts, none of which say they were delivered." My heart is breaking. I refuse to think that she could just disappear at a time like this, something must have happened. I can't think of a reason that she wouldn't have contacted me, but the idea that I might return home and have her gone is too much to bear. Clearing my throat, I lift a chair and move it so I can sit closer to her. "Let's just focus on my beautiful niece and the amazing job you did."

"I can't even believe it. I can't believe she's here. I can't believe I won the bet and Alex has to let me get her a miniature horse. I told him we were having a girl." Lia's attempt at a joke draws a small smile from me.

The little girl in her arms is too precious for words. She has a small amount of dark hair on her head, her chubby cheeks make her head super round.

"You guys are so lucky." The words are whispered. I want this for myself.

I sit with Lia for a while longer, lifting Stella from her arms and putting her in her bassinet when Lia's eyes start to close.

Slipping out of the room, I rejoin my family in the sitting room.

No one mentions Reese's absence, they know better, but I take my phone from Dad and check for some sort of contact.

Dialling Reese's number again, I resist the urge to throw my phone when it goes straight to voicemail. Did she block my number? What the actual fuck is going on?

"Son, remember to take a deep breath. You know Reese. You know she's not the type of person to disappear, so whatever is going on, she has a reason for it." Dad rests his hand over the fist that's clenching my phone.

He's saying exactly what I've been trying to tell myself, I just can't think of any feasible reason for disappearing right now.

Six hours. Reese left to go to the "bathroom" six hours ago. To be exact, six hours and thirteen minutes.

"Excuse me?" A nurse steps into the room, her eyes scanning my family. We're the only ones in here right now, but she's clearly looking for someone. "Is someone in here with a Reese?"

Standing, I walk over to her as my heart kicks into high gear. "I'm her boyfriend. What's going on?"

The nurse glances at the wide eyes of my family behind me and gestures for me to follow her into the hall.

"I found Reese in the bathroom, she was heaving and clutching her right side. We had to perform an emergency appendectomy on her." Her voice is low, rattling off the room number and waiting for me to repeat it. "She's out of surgery and awake. When I left about ten minutes ago she was in recovery waiting for the doctor."

Thanking her, I bolt into the waiting room. "Reese had appendicitis. I need to go see her, see for myself that she's okay. Please tell Lia and Alex."

They agree and I'm out of the waiting room before they can

ask questions that will prevent me from getting to Reese as quickly as possible.

As I race through the hallways, I curse the architect who designed this building. It's not intuitive as I work my way through the maze. Every hallway looks the same.

Two elevator rides and fifteen minutes later, I'm standing outside her room as a doctor steps out and closes the door behind him.

I can't believe I thought she could possibly have gone home to pack up and leave. She'd mentioned a stomach ache earlier and I'd definitely thought it was odd she didn't want to eat this morning. Now it all makes sense.

Taking a deep breath, I push my way into her room. There are four curtained off zones, none of which are open to see. Shit, I don't want to bother anyone. Stilling, I listen and hear a quiet sniffling behind the curtain immediately to my right.

Taking a chance, I slide it open enough so I can peek in. Reese's phone is clutched in one hand, tears streaking down her face. When her gaze meets mine, she lets out an anguished cry and starts sobbing.

Rushing to her side, I crouch down next to her and push some loose strands of hair back before taking her hand in mine. Her grip is tight, even with the trembling of her hand.

"Reese, what's wrong? I thought everything was okay?" My voice is a hoarse whisper, it scratches my throat.

She lifts her head, crying harder when she sees me. "I'm... so... sorry."

"What? No, it's okay. I understand it was an emergency. Lia's okay. She had a beautiful baby girl. Her name is Stella." Keeping my voice soothing, I panic when she just sobs harder.

Pulling her phone from her hand, I bite back an inappropriate chuckle when I see it's set to airplane mode. No wonder I couldn't get through.

Rubbing her back, I wait for her cries to calm a little before I get up and grab a chair, leaning in close as I wipe the tears away with my thumb. At times like these, I wish men still carried handkerchiefs like my grandfather, the hospital tissue is so paper thin and rough.

Reese takes a shaky breath, trying to calm her erratic breathing.

"I tried to tell you I was going into surgery. And I so wanted to be there. But... but..." She stops as she starts to cry again, closing her eyes and taking some more shaky breaths before she opens those beautiful hazel eyes and meets mine with a gaze so full of grief, I can feel it rock me. "After I woke up from my surgery, I noticed I was bleeding. A lot. And my stomach was cramping."

She takes in a shuddering breath, my heart jack hammering in my chest as I wait.

"The doctor—well"—her voice breaks as she bites back a whimper, her voice barely a whisper—"I had a miscarriage. I didn't know I was pregnant. I didn't know. And now the baby's gone. I lost it."

She starts crying again and I don't know what else to do as my mind completely freezes up. I don't let her hand go, running my thumb over the delicate skin as I try to catch up. My heart aching for the child now gone and the pain Reese is experiencing that I can't do anything to appease.

"Hey." I coo at her, "Shhh. You don't need to apologize, I'm so sorry I wasn't here with you when you got the news. I've got you."

"Because of my surgery they want me to follow up with my doctor for a check up. Honestly, I can't really remember every-thing they said, it's just so much. All I wanted was you." Her eyes close as she cries.

Standing, I carefully maneuver myself next to her and fold

her in my arms. "I'm here. I'm not going anywhere." Rubbing her back, I continue to coo at her until she falls asleep.

Holy. Shit.

I was going to be a father.

My eyes burn as I think about a baby born and one lost all in the same day. I know miscarriages happen. The statistic is quite high. Alex was researching it when he was worried about Lia riding while pregnant. Most women don't even know it happens because it happens so early.

I hold Reese as I watch her sleep. Her eyes are moving behind their lids and I can tell by her whimpers and moans she's not sleeping well.

Reaching between us, I take her hand and clutch it to my chest. One of the things Alex read in his research is that the loss of a baby can tear a couple apart. I cling to her and watch her as I vow not to let that happen.

I grieve for the baby we could've had, but I'm going to fight to show Reese that we can grieve this together, get past it, and, hopefully, one day, try again.

CHAPTER TWENTY-FOUR

Reese

It's been a week since I had my appendix out. Ryan rescheduled all our clients and he's been doting on me every moment. Some people may get fed up with the attention, but I've found comfort in his presence that I desperately need.

We haven't told anyone about the baby, I'm not ready. I know my sister went through this and I know she would try to alleviate my fears, but that's the thing about fear. It's relentless. Even when the rational part of your brain tells you everything will be okay, you wonder if it's lying to you. Many women face fertility issues. It's not as uncommon as people believe. What if I can't have children? What if my miscarriage is just a symptom of a larger issue?

The idea of not being able to have a family is devastating enough, the idea that it could create a rift with Ryan and eventually lead to me losing him, that's unbearable.

I've been trying to find it in me to tell him, to talk about it, but instead of doing what I know I should do, I hold it inside. I'll talk about it after my appointment with my new primary physician.

The door opens, a gust of cold air and some snow drifts in as Ryan and Luna come in from their walk. "It's freezing and the snow is really coming down, but the truck is swept off and running. I know you were planning on going to your appointment alone, but I thought I'd drive you and then, if you want, I can come in with you."

Stuffing my bookmark into the book I was attempting to read, I set it down and gingerly stand up. It's amazing the toll a simple surgery takes on one's body. I haven't had as much energy and I definitely feel it whenever I move.

"Okay." My agreement is soft. I know he's worried about me, I know he loves me, and I can feel his concern. I'm not trying to pull away, I just never knew I could feel an ache quite like this before.

He strides toward me, ignoring the snowy tracks he's leaving on the tile. Before I can protest, he chuckles. "I'll mop the floors when we get home." When he reaches me, he cups the back of my neck. "You're worrying me. I know a lot's going on and I know you're reeling from everything, but I need you to know it's going to be okay. We're going to be okay."

My heart jackhammers against my ribs as he gazes down at me. That same look that he always gives me, one of love and affection, one of home and forever and I finally voice my fears. "What if she finds a deeper issue? What if there's something wrong with me, something that makes it so we can't have children?"

Ryan pulls me into a hug and I don't even care that his jacket is cold because he knows exactly how to hold me so I feel safe and whole. "Then we adopt. Or we don't have kids and we choose a different path. We'll talk about it. We'll figure it out. We. You and me. That's not going to change."

He kisses the top of my head before stepping away to grab my coat. Once I'm all bundled, we make the thirty-minute drive into town.

If I can credit the doctor with one thing, it's that she's prompt. She's also the gentlest doctor I've ever had during a full physical and despite the sad bubble I've been living in, she managed to make me laugh a couple times.

She heads out of the room to pick up the requisition form for blood work and a urine sample, leaving me to change out of the paper gown and back into my clothes.

Ryan gives me a wicked grin as I strip it off. The incision from my surgery is healing nicely and I'm hoping in a week I'll get clearance to go back to work. The worst part about waiting a week to get an appointment is the fact I've been stuck inside my head.

Dr. Parsons knocks, stepping into the room with the paperwork.

"So, Reese, I know we discussed the miscarriage being a concern for you, so I want to discuss that first. Physically, I see no reason why getting pregnant will be an issue, whenever you're ready to try again. I want to reiterate that miscarriage, especially with a first pregnancy, is more common than people think. As soon as you're ready to return to regular activities, you could start trying again. I've requested several different tests that will help give a clearer picture. Our lab isn't very busy today, so if you have time they can take you in about twenty-minutes. If you don't hear from me within a few business days from the test, everything is fine." She smiles and hands me the paperwork.

My body relaxes and this time when I glance at Ryan, he waggles his eyebrows at me making me laugh.

"I do want to remind you that pregnancy after thirty-five increases your risks for complications, but as a healthy woman who is living a healthy lifestyle, I'm not concerned." She asks if I have any other questions, turning to Ryan when I don't. He shakes his head, standing and pulling me into his arms.

"I think we're good, thanks, Doc."

We say goodbye and she leaves the room.

We follow closely behind, holding hands as we head to the lab. Less than an hour later and we're on the road home again.

Now, all I need to do is wait and see if I hear from her before the end of the week, but I already feel lighter knowing she's not concerned.

"You know, there are ways we could start trying to get you pregnant again, ways that won't impact your incision." Ryan looks over at me with a saucy grin.

Smiling, I shift in my seat. "You don't think it's too soon?"

"You were already pregnant, what would you have done had you not lost the baby?" His tone is serious, his dark eyes searching mine.

"The same thing I'm doing now, except we'd have to decide which room in the house would be the baby's room." My voice fades at the end, his point becoming clear.

He smirks at me and I give him a small smile.

"I'm in. I don't want to wait." Hearing his words, I can't contain my smile. The fear of losing another baby will sit beneath the surface, but I can't imagine any woman who doesn't think about that risk to a certain extent. I just know that I want to start our family and I want to start it now.

CHAPTER TWENTY-FIVE

Ryan

Reese comes out of the bathroom of her apartment, her head shaking. My heart sinks when I see that familiar look of disappointment on her face. It's been two months since the doctor said there is no reason we couldn't get pregnant again, and nothing.

She navigates through the boxes littering the apartment floor, stepping into my waiting embrace. "It's okay. It will happen, we just need to be patient. And now that we're finally moving into your house—"

"Our house."

"Our house. We can focus on getting settled and just living. We've only been trying for a short time and I know it can take a while, so I'm going to quit testing because I don't want to get into that mindset at this point. If it hasn't happened for us in six months or a year, then we can explore tracking and all that." She plants a kiss on my chest, her words hopeful.

Hugging her close, I tilt her head back and kiss her, never tiring of the way her lips feel on mine. Tonight we'll be spending our first night in our home. The house was done mid-March, as projected, but we agreed to wait to move in until we'd carefully selected furniture and décor to fill the space. It took a month of searching, countless hours spent online trying to find small, boutique stores that carried handmade furniture and unique pieces to fit the feel that we wanted, but it's finally ready.

"I think that sounds perfect. You know, Mom had two miscarriages prior to getting pregnant with me and then it took them almost two years before she got pregnant with Dane. The doctor said it could take time." Smiling as she pulls away, nodding, I remember talking to Mom about everything, opening up about the miscarriage and Reese's fear. My fear.

It's hard to turn that off once it happens. It's hard not to wonder if it will happen again, but her story helped me and I can tell that it helps Reese.

Michelle has also been incredible, I finally convinced Reese to talk to her about it, especially since she had so much trouble with pregnancy and chose to only conceive once due to the risks.

Since then Reese has been more optimistic about our chances.

We part, eyeing the boxes around us. There aren't too many, and this is our last stop of the day. We make quick work of loading them into the back of my pickup truck and once we're parked inside the garage, we're surrounded by our family who all assembled to help.

Since both of us only had our clothes and small personal items, it hasn't taken long to move everything and put the boxes into the appropriate rooms.

Instead of unpacking, we convene in the kitchen for an amazing lunch courtesy of our mothers.

"So, I know this is Reese and Ryan's day, but I spoke with Reese yesterday and she told me to go ahead and share," Emma begins, her eyes shining. "I just found out a few weeks ago I'm pregnant!"

Reaching over I squeeze Reese's hand as I congratulate Emma. She glances over at me and smiles, genuine joy written all over her face.

Every day she continues to amaze me. She's so generous and kind, not letting her own stuff impact her joy when others have good news.

We toast, Emma lifting a glass of sparkling peach juice, something she's apparently been craving.

Once everyone is gone for the night, I sweep Reese into my arms and carry her up the stairs. Kicking the door shut to our room, I direct Luna to her basket before laying Reese onto our king size bed.

"I love you. I can't wait to share my life with you and build this house into a home." Dropping down I kiss her, ready to lose myself in her arms.

"Forever," she whispers.

EPILOGUE

Four Months Later

Reese

Blinking as I look down, my heart starts to pound. No, this can't be right.

Except all four have said the same thing.

Pregnant.

Holy. Shit.

I'm pregnant.

I can't get out of the bathroom quick enough, seriously, how long does it take for soap to rinse off? And where is my hand towel?

Racing down the steps and onto the porch, I skid to a stop when I see Ryan laughing with Dane and Alex.

While, I love the idea of doing something cute to announce

to him that I'm pregnant, there's no way I can contain myself long enough to think of something creative.

"Ryan." I bound down the steps, ignoring the dirt on my bare feet as I run toward him, the pregnancy test clutched in my hand as I wave it in the air. "You're going to be a daddy!"

The End

Read more by Ashley Erin

Sign up for my Newsletter